A Haunted
MASQUERADE

A HAUNTED MASQUERADE

A GHOSTLY GEORGIAN FAIRY TALE RETELLING

E.B. WHEELER

Rowan Ridge
Press

ISBN: 978-1-960033-12-3

First printing: November 2023

Published by Rowan Ridge Press, Utah

Cover image © heckmannoleg

Cover design © Rowan Ridge Press

For the dreamers and the doers

CHAPTER I

The pale cliffs of England glowed behind the midnight swells of the channel. Stars peeked through gashes in the fast-moving clouds, winking at me with their secrets, but I ignored them. My father had lost himself chasing those secrets, and I had not been able to save him. Now, it was only my brother Henri and me and whatever hope waited for us beyond those steep cliffs.

I gripped the rail of the little boat slipping through the dark waters. The sea spray brushed my face with a salty chill, and the wind tangled my short, curly locks. I had traded my voluminous skirts for trousers to flee Paris, and the lack of fabric left me vulnerable, more exposed to the cold touch of the night. But safety was almost within reach.

A light blinked from the cliffs, reminding me of the flash of the guillotine. I shuddered and turned away. Where was Henri? My younger brother had an uncomfortable habit of wandering off.

I only went a few steps before Henri found me. He scurried up, his cravat disarrayed and his narrow face more pale than usual. A familiar worry wormed its way around my stomach.

"Henri?" I kept my voice low. "What have you been doing?"

"We have a bit of money to get us through, don't we, Charlotte—er, Charles?" he whispered, using the false name that went with my disguise of trousers and a waistcoat.

My eyes narrowed. "A little, once we pay the captain the rest of his share. But we can't count on father's cousins. We're going to have to find work. Well, I will." Henri had never been strong enough for hard work, and after months of dodging citizen militias and scrambling through the countryside, he looked as fragile as a bone china plate.

"I can help you," he said, trying to puff out his thin chest. "You'll see that I can. I'll pay you back."

My stomach lurched. "Pay me back?"

"You see, I've been playing cards with the sailors. I thought I could make us a few extra shillings, but the cards didn't turn my way."

I shut my eyes, swallowing a sick feeling. "How much?"

"The stakes ran a little high. Five pounds."

"Five!" I reached back for the unsteady support of the ship's railing. That was far more than all the coin we had. "Please tell me you didn't."

"Well, not exactly. You see, I had such good cards. I challenged them to double it."

"Ten?" My lips formed the word, but the sound didn't come out.

"I'm sorry, Charles. Really, I am."

I turned back to the sea, trying not to lose my dinner over the side of the ship. I could shake my brother for his rashness. But, no, this was my fault. I should have watched him more carefully.

"We don't have it," I whispered, clutching the hidden purse that held our last copper sous and deniers, mingled with an odd shilling or two. Even if I sold everything we had, the clothes we wore, we did not have ten pounds.

"But, then what will we do?" Henri asked.

"Maybe the captain will understand," I said.

Henri was just a youth, after all. A sickly one at that. Though, maybe not *such* a youth anymore. He was fourteen. Young enough to be a fool, but old enough to be held accountable for it.

"Understand what?" came the captain's gruff voice.

I spun to face the grizzled old man. Before I could gather my thoughts, Henri poured out his imprudent tale, his eyes pleading for understanding.

The captain stared down at the both of us, then leveled his gaze on Henri. "If you don't have the money you owe my crew, you'll have to work it off."

"W-work it off?" Henri stammered.

"That could take a year or more!" I said.

The captain shrugged. "Debts must be paid."

"Sir," I said, remembering to pitch my voice low. "My brother has never been very healthy."

"Then I hope ten pounds worth of hard work toughens him up."

"But..." I looked helplessly at Henri, who turned his

frightened gaze on me. He might be fourteen, but those were the eyes of the boy who had cried and clung to me when he was ill and had no mother to comfort him, who asked what we were to do when Father was arrested.

"I will work beside him, then," I said.

"I only have room for one ship's boy." The captain looked between us, then settled his gaze on me. "Between the two, I'd rather have you. You're heartier. You stay to pay the debt, and I'll let the boy go ashore."

Henri grasped my arm.

"What if I worked for you on shore?" I asked. "There must be something I could do, and then Henri could stay with me."

"In my line of work, the fewer people who know my business, the better. I already have all the contacts I want in town. What I need is a lad to work around the ship."

Something hot stirred in my belly. Had the captain planned this, hoping to force one of us to work for him? He had allowed his men to gamble with a destitute boy and take advantage of his naivety, at the least. But there was no one to complain to, no one who cared what became of two orphans fleeing the Terror. Anger flared and died as quickly as the flash of a blade. I had to resolve this myself.

My fast-beating pulse echoed in my ears, and I looked to Henri. If I stayed on board, the crew would eventually discover I was a girl. And what would they do to me then? But I couldn't let them work Henri to death.

"I'll stay," I said, the words thick and ashy in my mouth.

"Don't send me ashore alone," Henri pleaded with me. "I don't know how to find our cousins."

Our cousins! A new possibility warmed me, and I faced the captain. "We have relatives in England. Possibly here in Lymouth. Surely, they'll pay the debt."

The captain shrugged. "Then one of you can find them and bring me the money next month. We make port in Lymouth every new moon. But the other has to stay to make certain I'm paid."

One month. Henri would be lost onshore, alone for so long. And I had no guarantees our cousins were in Lymouth this season. How would Henri work his way through England looking for them? At least on the ship, he would be fed. I didn't see a way around it. Henri had to stay while I went.

"I will find the money and return for you in one month," I said to Henri, forcing my voice to stay level.

A gleam of trust lit Henri's eyes. My stomach lurched, though the sea was calm.

The captain grunted. "I'll make what use I can of him in the meanwhile."

I embraced Henri, who shivered as though the salty wind would tatter him like a wet paper. He had barely survived birth, while our mother had succumbed. Ever since, I had been the one to keep him alive, with Father too lost in his telescopes and microscopes. I had promised Mother—and then Father—that I would take care of Henri. I squeezed his hand, memorizing the warmth of his fragile, uncalloused fingers.

The captain's rough grip landed on my shoulder. "Time to go."

"No!"

I tried to hold onto Henri, but the captain dragged me from my brother and practically tossed me into the rowboat where his men loaded their cargo.

"Charlie!" Henri cried, stretching out his hand.

My heart lurched, and I reached back. "One month. I will free you!"

The captain climbed into the boat and forced me to sit. I huddled between trunks and barrels I didn't want to know the contents of. In our hurry to leave France, I had not asked questions about the legality of the ship's nighttime runs across the English Channel. Now, I watched the tiny ship and my brother grow smaller.

"I'll put you ashore a distance from my rendezvous," the captain said, keeping his voice low. "You still may see or hear things tonight. You would do best not to notice any faces and to be forgetful about the details of our transactions. Above all, avoid the revenue men."

I nodded grudgingly. Any trouble for the captain would mean trouble for Henri as well.

After a choppy ride across the breakers, the rowboat approached a rocky stretch of shore.

"There's a path to town up the cliffs here," the captain said.

As Charlotte, the men would have offered me a hand out of the boat, but in my boy's guise, I was left to scramble out of the boat with an inelegant splash. The cold water shoved at my unsteady legs.

I faced the captain and raised my voice to be heard over the waves breaking on the shore. "If he's not alive and well when we meet next month, you get nothing."

And I would make certain the revenue men found him.

The captain returned a curt nod.

I sloshed through the surf to the damp sand. Now, I was grateful for my trousers, since a wet skirt would have been a severe impediment. And young ladies were very limited in the work they could find—maid or seamstress were the more pleasant possibilities. Young men, however, could run about town and find a variety of jobs. Charlotte or Charles: what did it matter who I was as long as I saved my brother?

Without another word, the boat's oars splashed in the surf, and I was alone. Well, I hadn't been expecting a hearty farewell from the smugglers. But I had been expecting to arrive here with Henri. I looked back toward the boat and my brother, but the darkness hid them from me. I swallowed a lump in my throat and turned to face England.

Remembering what the captain said about not seeing too much, I hurried up the path to the top of the cliffs. The ruins of some ancient church or monastery looked out over the sea, and I stopped there to catch my breath. The distant flicker of lamps showed me the way to Lymouth.

My father had a cousin, Mr. Medford, who liked to spend the autumn season in Lymouth. It was why I'd sought a boat heading for the seaside town. I had no guarantee that Medford was here, or that he'd help me, but I would humble myself and beg for help if I could find him. If that failed, I would work as a servant. It was below the station I was born to—the daughter of a gentleman-scientist and a French lady—but thanks to my mother's death and my father's absent-mindedness, I knew how to work hard. Though, it might take me a year to make ten pounds as a servant, while Henri sailed the rough winter seas with smugglers.

I imagined Henri growing weak and dying, his body sewn into a ragged scrap of sail and tossed into the sea for a sailor's burial. The last of my family dead. The ground swayed beneath me, and I stumbled. No, I could not allow that.

One thing worked in my favor: seaside towns like Lymouth brimmed with wealthy people. There had to be work for me here. My family had visited England so my father could confer with other natural scientists before the troubles overtook France, so I had some idea of how to interact with the English, and I was fluent in their beastly language.

I hurried past farms on the outskirts of town. Growing up in Paris, I knew little about agriculture, but perhaps I could learn. The farms gave way to snug cottages—probably the homes of fishermen—and then to tall, narrow houses and inns rubbing shoulders with each other, their windows curtained as if they slept along with their inhabitants. An assembly hall overlooking the sea provided a place for weekly dancing. A tug of regret reminded me that the balls and parties would not be for me.

I should have been frightened, a young woman wandering the streets alone, but I was dressed as a young man, and after all I had seen in France, England did not seem so dangerous.

I paused on the street, looking up to an open bedroom window in an inn. I remembered something about English law: breaking a window to rob a house was a hangable offense, but taking something from an open window was a less serious crime. I didn't want to be a thief, but neither did I want to leave my brother a captive. I had gleaned from French farmer's fields and even stolen from their orchards and barns to feed Henri and myself after we fled Paris. The boys' clothes I wore came from some wealthy landowner's neglected laundry basket. An aching stomach, my brother's protruding ribs, and the muskets of citizen militias had shown me I was capable of many things I had never imagined for myself.

"Not worth it," slurred a male voice behind me.

I spun, heart pounding. A young man in a high-collared shirt and intricate cravat stood there, staring up at the window with a quizzing glass. His face was handsome in a sharp way, his golden hair unpowdered and showing hints of red in the light from the inn.

"Pardon?" I choked out.

"Knowing Martin, you either want to collect a debt or murder him in his sleep, and either way, he's not in. I left him snoring off his drinks at Goring's." The young man's green eyes flashed with amusement. "Besides, I already robbed him, and now I'm left with his vowels."

"His vowels?" I asked. The man had been drinking, but he didn't seem so far gone that he would be unintelligible.

"Ah, you are French. I hear it now. Yes, his vowels: his IOU. He has nothing left to take."

"And you robbed him?" I was struck by amazement that English gentlemen spoke of crime so casually.

"Playing cards with him when he was foxed was practically robbing him. The man was too deep in his cups to count his cards. But I can't be responsible for everyone else's bad decisions. I have enough of my own to occupy me." He hesitated, swaying a little. "I suppose he owed you money, too, and you wished to retrieve it? I hope you did not need it too urgently."

"I did." I sighed, thinking of all the coins wealthy and drunk young men tossed around while Henri scrubbed decks and coiled ropes until his hands bled.

The man frowned and dug into his pocket. He tossed me a coin that flashed yellow in the light. "Take this as an apology that I made you wait that much longer."

I gawked at the gold coin in my palm. A guinea! My heart swelled with hope. Fortune had thus far not shown me much favor, but perhaps England would change my luck. A few more encounters with drunk gentlemen, and I might have enough to free Henri in a week.

"Thank you! Can you tell me if Mr. Medford is in Lymouth this year?"

"Ah, if he owed you money, too, you're much too late."

The warm flare of hope dimmed. "What do you mean?"

"He's dead, these two years past."

"Oh." No helpful cousin awaited me, then. I clutched the coin, chilly against my fingers, and the cold seeped through me, a dreary weight that made me want to curl up and hide from guillotines, smugglers, and gambling debts.

The young man pointed down the street. "His widow is visiting with her daughters, but you will not find her friendly to debt collectors. Her husband's death left her with a thin purse, and her every breath is in service to marrying off those horrid girls. She doesn't tolerate distractions."

I frowned over that. Mrs. Medford wouldn't have money to spare for Henri then. Would she offer me a place to stay, at least? References for work? I had to ask.

I turned to thank the man again, but he had already wandered off. I tucked the gold guinea into the purse with my remaining coins. The guinea was a good start, but I needed to earn more. I wasn't likely to be that lucky again, and I didn't want the watch to find me lurking in the streets.

I wandered down to the house the young man had indicated. It was a solid, three-story building painted white so it looked cold and hard against the soft darkness of the night.

Someone moved in the attic. A servant working late? It looked like a young woman staring out into the street as though seeking something. Her face was pinched with worry —or fear. Was she in trouble? Held against her will? I didn't know all the laws of England, but I was fairly certain they couldn't do that to servants.

When I looked again, the young woman was gone. Certainly, she was not one of the daughters seeking a husband—not if she was in the attic—though she had been young and pretty. I remembered what the blond man had said about distractions. Would a young, pretty servant girl be a distraction, kept out of sight?

If that were the case, Mrs. Medford would not want another young woman in the house, even a cousin. I wasn't seeking a husband—who would want a penniless orphan girl?—and so I wasn't competition for her daughters, but I might be in the way. I glanced down at my boy's clothing.

Unless I were a male cousin. Then, I could help the girls, escorting them to balls or scouting out potential suitors. I did not think the Medfords knew enough of my family to realize Charles should be Charlotte. So, Charles would continue to serve me well, at least until Henri was free.

CHAPTER 2

I decided that my father's cousins couldn't begrudge me one night of free hospitality. An alley ran beside the house to stables in the back. Six months earlier, I wouldn't have considered climbing over the low stone wall into the rear garden, but now I scrambled over it with ease. The overgrown, neglected hedges confirmed what the gentleman had said about Mrs. Medford's purse being thin, but they did make it easier to hide.

I found a garden folly in the shape of a small, rectangular Roman temple. With walls on three sides and a front portico guarded by columns, it wouldn't be the worst place I had spent a night since they arrested Father. At least its plastered white roof sheltered me from the clouds and stars. I curled up on the chilly cement floor, cushioned my head on the crook of my elbow, and dozed until the song of birds welcomed the impending dawn.

Waking in the shadows of the stone columns gave me a

momentary sense of imprisonment, and the sound of tumbrel wheels rumbling from the Conciergerie to the Place de la Révolution echoed in my mind.

I shook off the weight of dread and turned to a decrepit pear tree for an underripe breakfast. My mouth watered at the crisp, tart fruit, and my stomach ached for more. Even if Mrs. Medford sent me on my way, I would beg for breakfast first.

A bronze angel holding a shallow bowl filled with rainwater served as my dressing table and mirror. I winced at my pinched, sun-tanned face and the disorder of my short, curly hair. Was this really how I looked now? I had never been a great beauty, with my thin frame and unruly locks, and Father had been too busy with his studies to take us to many social events where I might wear silk or jewels, but I had been a respectable young lady.

None of which mattered anymore.

I was never one of those sparkling ladies meant for ballrooms and salons and being courted by handsome gentlemen. The reminder stabbed me with a longing I hardly dared admit even to myself. No. I was useful and resourceful. That was all. That was why Henri and I were still alive.

I took a moment to become better acquainted with "Charles." My trousers, waistcoat, and jacket were nowhere near as fine as the drunk gentleman's, but they were respectable enough, especially once I brushed off a few stray brown leaves. I finger-combed my hair into some semblance of order and straightened my cravat, hiding the dirty spots as well as I could. I wouldn't show up on my cousins' steps looking like the beggar I was. And if they turned me away, I might pass for an errand boy. That would let me earn some coin while I looked for more opportunities to fill my purse.

I scrambled over the garden wall and approached the front door to knock.

After a long wait, a middle-aged butler answered the door. He frowned at me, obviously not sure what to make of the boy on the front steps. At least he didn't send me directly to the back door with the servants.

"I am Charles Carter, cousin to the late Mr. Medford. I have come to pay a visit to his widow."

I didn't try to disguise my French accent. I hoped it would make me seem interesting, if not respectable.

The butler looked me up and down with some skepticism, but he finally said, "Very well. Right this way...sir."

He showed me to a drawing room hung with red drapes. Despite the early morning light filtering through the windows, ominous shadows crowded the corners. Perhaps the room was meant to intimidate me, but I couldn't let anything frighten me away from saving Henri.

I paced the room, then eventually sat on a red sofa. Maybe Mrs. Medford wasn't even awake yet. Maybe the butler conveniently forgot me and hoped I would go away. If I had wanted to rob someone, this might be an excellent way to do it. Not that the room offered anything worth stealing: a few cheap ornaments and some uninspired sketches on the walls. A rented lodging for the season.

A rented lodging with too much red. Almost the color of blood. What a tasteless choice. I tried not to stare at the cascade of the red draperies. Falling across the light like a waterfall of blood. It filled my vision, my mind, my nose, until I choked on it. The blood of commoners and nobles alike mingled, and you couldn't tell one from the other. And I watched from the back of the crowd, helpless to stop any of it. It was a flood of dark red, and all I could do was try to keep it from staining my shoes or splattering my clothes. Beneath the hoarse, bestial shouts of the crowd, someone was weeping. Was it Henri? He needed to stay quiet, stay hidden.

I stood and stepped toward the weeping.

The vision of red faded, but the weeping continued. I tilted my head to listen, remembering the girl I had seen in the attic the night before. Finally, when the crying didn't stop and no one else responded, I dared to open the door and creep down the corridor to an adjoining sitting room.

The crying was definitely coming from behind that door. The sound turned from delicate sniffling to a gush of sobs. I hesitated outside the door, but it swung open as I stepped up to it, as though welcoming me. I peeked in.

A pale young lady with black hair sprawled on the sofa—yellow, this time—taking rasping breaths and dabbing her face with a handkerchief. Not the brown-haired girl I had seen the night before. Even with her eyes red from crying, this young lady was an English beauty, though.

Without thinking, I hurried to her side.

"Mademoiselle, are you injured?" I turned to the corridor. "Help!"

She stared up at me with her luminescent brown eyes and drew a shaky breath. "Oh! You are French. Are you the new tutor?"

I wrinkled my forehead at this non sequitur. "Are you

feverish? What has happened to you? Perhaps you need to sit up?"

"No, it will do no good," she whispered.

"How can I help you?"

"I am beyond help!" she wailed. "I have been shamed, and I shall never recover. Please, speak to me in French. Your accent will calm me."

Bemused, I stammered out a nursery story my mother used to tell me. The girl's breathing grew more even as I spoke. A forgotten tea tray caught my eye, and I grabbed a scone to satiate my hunger.

"What is this, Frances?" asked a soft feminine voice from the doorway. "Who are you?"

I glanced up to see a calmer version of the girl on the sofa carrying a vial of smelling salts. And I remembered that I was dressed as a boy. I should not have been alone with a young lady. This would be the moment they threw me onto the streets.

"Do not interrupt, Loretta," the girl on the sofa—Frances —scolded. "Our new tutor knows just how to soothe me."

"You are a tutor?" Loretta asked.

Her voice wasn't harsh, but her skepticism was obvious. No wonder. I was almost twenty, but as a boy, I looked no older than sixteen.

"I have just come from France," I said. "I am Charles Carter. I believe we are cousins."

"Cousins?" Loretta asked, interest lighting her weary eyes.

"Mama told me she would find a new tutor." Frances pouted.

Loretta sighed and knelt beside Frances. "I'm certain Mother will find us a tutor." She glanced at me apologetically. "Mother has trouble finding us tutors who are..."

"Who are not too boorish," Frances said. "Why are all men such beasts?"

She lapsed back into tears.

Loretta gave me an apologetic look. "She had an...unfortunate encounter last night at a ball."

"Lord Martin said nothing would induce him to marry me, even if I had a king's fortune—which I do not!" Frances gasped between sobs. "And everyone heard. Some of them laughed!"

"That's beastly!" I said. Even if a gentleman didn't want to marry such a...sensitive girl, he should not have publicly embarrassed her.

"And I have no male relative to take my part—" Frances broke off and gave me a speculative look. "But you are my cousin. Perhaps if you dueled Lord Martin, it would restore me from my shame."

I gaped at her. "Uh, I am...not trained as a duelist, I'm afraid."

Was Martin not the name of the man whom the blond gentleman had "robbed" at cards? At least there had been a measure of justice served against Martin, then.

Frances's eyes flashed. "I thought all Frenchmen were hotblooded. Or is that Italians? But it cannot be so hard to shoot a pistol. I would like to do it myself."

"Frances!" said a woman from the doorway. "You should not overexcite yourself so."

I looked to see a dark-haired older woman—obviously

the mother or aunt of the girls—watching us. A necklace glittered at her throat, displaying a garnet the color of blood.

She eyed me narrowly. "So, you are the young man who claims to be a cousin to my late husband?"

I stood and bowed. "Charles Carter. My father was Frederick Carter, the natural scientist."

"Charles is our cousin," Frances said. "Tell him he must duel Lord Martin for me!"

The woman sighed and knelt beside her daughter's sofa. "It would not do to have your name bandied about in such lurid circumstances, my dear." She addressed me. "I recall that Mr. Medford had a cousin who had gone to France and married a French wife. And now I suppose he is back."

Her tone suffocated any hope that my father's cousins would make me welcome. No matter. I had grown accustomed to being overlooked, and at least I knew how to make myself useful.

"My father is dead, madam," I said as levelly as I could. "And I have come back to England."

Loretta looked at me with sympathy, but Mrs. Medford sniffed skeptically.

"If you are seeking money, I have none to spare."

I took a deep breath. "I understand that, madam. I did hope I might find shelter under your roof for a time, but I plan to make my own way in England. I will not be a burden."

"Hmm," Mrs. Medford replied.

"He told me the loveliest children's story, Mother," Frances said. "It was soothing to my nerves."

Mrs. Medford gave me a sharp look. "You have no

designs on my daughters, I hope! They have much loftier ambitions than a poor French cousin."

My cheeks reddened, and I had to stifle a laugh. "I am not seeking a wife, lovely as my cousins are. But if you wish for someone to practice French with them, I would be happy to oblige."

"Oh, let him stay, Mother," Frances said. "He amuses me."

Mrs. Medford sighed. "Very well. It is a Christian thing to give émigrés a fresh start in England, and I am a good, charitable woman, as anyone will tell you. Though, I will keep a close eye on you, Cartier."

And with that, my father's English "Carter" became the French "Cartier." Yet I didn't dare contradict her when so much depended on her grudging charity.

"I'm not sure you understand English expectations of behavior," Mrs. Medford went on, "so I will be clear: We will take you in as a tutor—a servant, not a member of the household. Your origins give you access to this house—and to my daughters—only in that capacity."

"Yes, madam, of course," I said hastily.

A calculating gleam entered her eyes. "What can you teach besides French?"

"I am experienced in the sciences and in sketching." Those thanks to helping my father with his work.

"The girls have no use for science, but sketching would be a pleasant pastime for them." She turned her back on me to smooth Frances's hair. "We are not using the attic. You may sleep there."

"Thank you, madam," I said sincerely.

I had a solution to my need of shelter. It was a start. I was curious about the face I had seen in the attic window, though, if they weren't using the space.

"But Mama," Frances said in a stage whisper. "The servants won't go in there because of the strange noises."

I raised my eyebrows at that.

"Nonsense. Don't fret yourself child." The lady turned to me. "We shall have French lessons each day after nuncheon. Since we are providing for you, I expect you to assist the dance master and the music tutor when they come. And perhaps you can also teach some literature and geography?"

"Yes, madam," I said. "I'm fluent in English, French, and German, and I have an excellent understanding of geography."

One of the few things my father had not neglected was arranging excellent tutors for Henri and me. Father would never have dreamed of me using my education to dress as a young man and teach English girls, but if he even noticed, he would have been glad I was surviving, and more importantly, that I would be able to help Henri.

CHAPTER 3

Loretta guided me to the attic, silent as a shadow, though she cast many curious glances my way. Rugs softened our footsteps as we climbed the stairs, and a strange stillness embraced the house, broken only by the occasional clatter of a carriage outside. We didn't pass any servants. The house seemed understaffed, but perhaps that was the way of the English when visiting the seaside.

"It is interesting to have a cousin," I finally said. "Living in France, I only had an old aunt on my mother's side, and she went to live in a convent."

My voice sounded too loud in the high-ceilinged corridor.

Loretta fixed me with a speculative look before responding. "Yes, it is interesting. I'm sorry your father is gone, and we never had a chance to meet him."

I nodded my thanks for her condolences. "I am sorry about your father as well."

Her gaze fell. "It has been difficult for all of us. Especially Frances. She suffers. Coming to Lymouth where we spent many happy days with Father helps her, though."

I thought of Henri with a wrenching in my chest. "It is difficult to have a younger sibling who is unwell."

Loretta looked at me in surprise. "Oh, Frances is older than me. And it is not that she is sickly, only that she is given much to nervous troubles. Her constitution was always delicate, and the shock of losing Father and...and the security he provided has brought her low."

Yes, losing a father could cast a family from comfort to poverty in a moment. The specter of hunger and homelessness was a terrible companion.

"I'm sorry," I whispered. "That must have been devastating."

She swallowed hard. "Yes."

We paused at the final flight of stairs. Loretta looked to the attic door at the top, and her pale skin went linen-white.

She rested a hesitant hand on the railing, then quickly pulled it away. "We don't go up there often. We only leased the house for the season, you see. We were fortunate it was available, but we don't know it well, and sometimes it feels... unwelcoming to me. As if it misses its former occupants." She bit her lip. "That must sound silly."

I smiled. "Not at all. I can find my way. Thank you."

She smiled back weakly and hurried away. After the terror I had seen in France, whatever was in the attic didn't frighten me, but I was curious. What if someone was hiding up there, another castaway like me?

I took the stairs quickly and swung the door open.

Silence greeted me. Glittering motes floated in the beams of weak light from the little windows. I waved them away. Dust lay over the floor, and I searched for footprints or any signs of human occupation, but there wasn't even a trace of mice.

"Hello?" I asked.

Nothing. It was empty, of course. Maybe I had only seen a strange reflection in the window.

I wandered the attic, trying to make myself at home. The slanted ceiling forced me to duck my head as I examined many worn pieces of furniture, including a bed that didn't look too uncomfortable. Otherwise, the long room was stuffed with old trunks and other forgotten things, probably left behind by former tenants.

I opened the windows to dispel some of the dust and pushed trunks and moth-eaten carpets away from the bed. The straw in the mattress tick had gone musty, but at least it also contained some wool. I pounded the mattress tick to revive it, and dust tickled my nose and filled my throat. I sneezed violently several times.

"God bless you," came a response so quiet I might have imagined it.

I rubbed the dust from my eyes and looked around the room. Nothing moved. My gaze rested on the open window. Had someone outside heard me sneeze?

A chill passed over me, and goosebumps rose along my arms. I rubbed them and frowned at my makeshift boudoir. I was going to need a blanket at the least, and none in the attic would be fit to keep anyone warm.

I trotted back downstairs, leaving the door open to better

freshen up the attic. The main floors of the house felt cozy in comparison to my new lodgings, but I was grateful to have a place to sleep. Not seeing any maids about, I found the linen closet near the bedrooms myself.

"What are you doing?" Mrs. Medford snapped from behind me.

I turned, clutching a blanket. "It is cold in the attic, madam."

She shut her eyes and pinched the bridge of her nose. "And so, you go rummaging through our closets? You are fortunate that my girls have taken a liking to you, and that I am so indulgent."

I wasn't certain of the correct response. "Thank you?"

She looked at me again and wrinkled her nose. "You're filthy. Do you want to shame this household?"

I looked down at my clothes, which had not been very clean even before I started on the attic. "I'm sorry. I'm afraid I fled France without anything else to wear."

"Oh, don't sound so dramatic." Mrs. Medford waved a hand at me. "I can't be responsible for outfitting every poor relative who shows up at my front door. Check the trunks in the attic. I'm certain some have serviceable clothing. You can use whatever you find up there, so long as you don't go around looking like a beggar."

"Thank you!" I said, sincerely this time.

Because she had given me an idea.

I took my blanket back to the attic. The door was shut, and I had to rattle the handle and push with my shoulder to open it. No doubt the breeze from the windows had blown it closed. I tossed the blanket on the bed and shut the windows.

Then I turned to look at the trunks. They were abandoned, and Mrs. Medford had said I could use whatever I found in them. These trunks might contain something I could pawn or sell to pay off my brother's debt. That wasn't what Mrs. Medford had intended, of course, and the trunks didn't really belong to her, but the people who left them behind owned so much that they didn't miss these things. Was it really stealing if no one would even notice?

Yes, I supposed it was, but if I found another source of money, I could buy the things back later. And here I was arranging my bed and thinking of my own scruples while my brother might be dying on a smuggling ship. That ship was supposed to return in a month, but what if the fortunes of the smugglers changed after that and they decided next to go to the West Indies or Tahiti? I had to rescue my brother before he was lost to me forever.

The first trunk I opened had ancient clothing in very poor repair. Nothing I could sell unless I wanted to strip off some of the trimmings. It might come to that. It was unlikely that anyone would leave behind jewels or anything truly valuable.

Another trunk answered one of my immediate problems. It held more boys' clothing: clean white shirts and a few waistcoats. With a bit of modification, they would suit me. The tight-fitting English breeches might reveal too much, but I could wash my looser French trousers and at least be able to change shirts.

I gathered some of the old dresses to pick off the trimmings. The space between my shoulder blades itched like someone was watching me, but of course, I was alone. I rolled my shoulders. It was probably my guilt nagging at me, but I silenced it for Henri's sake.

An ancient dressing table with a wobbly leg provided scissors for the trimmings, some thread, and even a mirror. I studied myself again. How strange would it be for a boy to bring women's clothing to a secondhand shop? Fairly suspicious. But I might find a dress I could wear in one of the trunks. A young woman pawning old clothes would look less odd.

I sorted through a trunk of moth-eaten shawls and then one with wigs, some high and powdered, and others less conspicuous. The powdered ones might be valuable, though they had fallen out of fashion as the heads that once wore them in France dropped into bloody baskets. Of course, the guillotine's victims went to their deaths with heads shorn and necks bare to welcome the blade. Father had never worn elaborate wigs, but he had looked like a stranger with his graying hair cut short.

I shuddered and shoved the more elaborate wigs aside, my hands shaking. Think of Henri. Anything to save him. I swallowed the lump in my throat and sorted through the wigs. A few of the simpler ones might be useful for disguising myself, but the rest I could sell.

A scraping noise brought me to a halt. I looked up, but the attic was still, and I was alone. Prickles ran over my skin. What had I heard? A noise on the roof, perhaps?

A small trunk set apart from the others caught my attention. Had it been there before?

I opened it, revealing clothes in good condition and fit for a young lady. A pair of red fabric dancing slippers adorned with feathers sat atop the dresses. How odd. English fashion was beyond my comprehension. The clothes in the trunk appeared only a year or two behind the latest mode. I wondered what became of the young lady who once wore them. Hopefully, she married a kind and handsome gentleman she met at one of the dances in Lymouth and happily left behind these vestiges of her maidenhood.

I selected a corset and a relatively plain dress I could wear to sneak down to the secondhand shops. I wouldn't look like a servant girl stealing her mistress's clothes, but I would not appear so elegant as to draw attention.

I gathered several dresses and wigs I could sell, along with my new disguise. I saw no reason to hesitate at this opportunity in case fortune snatched it away from me. But where was I to change? I couldn't be caught in the house as a girl, and I couldn't wait for the cover of darkness or the shops would be closed.

I glanced out the tiny back window at the roof of the miniature Roman temple. It was not very visible from the house thanks to the overgrown bushes, and its three walls would hide me from any curious neighbors. I could dress there.

I bundled the clothes under my arm and opened the attic door. When I did, a breeze blew through the room from the loosely-fitting windows. Almost like a ghostly sigh of *stay*. I shivered. My imagination was running away with me. After all, if spirits lingered on earth, why did my father's ghost not return to warn us or protect us? Why had my mother been silent all these years?

I shook off my morbid thoughts and hurried down the stairs and into the garden with my bundle of clothes, avoiding anyone from the household. Sheltered in the Roman folly, I stripped off my boys' clothes, trading them for the gown. That was another thing I had become adept at: dressing and adjusting my lacings without help. I had been pleased at my ability to take care of myself and Henri on my own. But I had nothing to boast about until my brother was free.

It felt both liberating and restricting to trade trousers for skirts. I sat for a moment, taking slow breaths and reminding myself that I was a young lady again. Then I stood, proper and full of composure, and placed a blonde wig over my short curls. Of course, I had no explanation for why I was in the garden as a stranger. I found a back gate and hurried out, keeping my head down so no one would recognize me as I scurried up the alley.

In front of the house, I slammed directly into someone.

I gasped and looked up, right into the face of the man who had tossed me the guinea the night before.

Except, he was so different now, he might almost have been another person. He sneered down at me, his sharp features set in bored annoyance. His eyes caught mine, and his brow creased slightly. I immediately felt foolish for slamming into him, but I was afraid if I spoke, he would remember my accent. So, I settled for glaring at him and hurrying away.

I could feel his stare as I continued at a brisk—but feminine—pace.

"Treverton!" another man called.

I glanced back to see him turn away, and my heartbeat finally slowed. I would get the money from the secondhand clothing store, slip back into my male clothes, and no one would be the wiser.

CHAPTER 4

I returned from the pawnbroker and the secondhand shop, my coin pouch jingling with lovely English money. The proprietors hadn't batted an eye at me selling an assortment of wigs and clothing. I might have even gone dressed as Charles without any trouble. The woman at the secondhand shop probably took advantage of my naivety about shillings and pence, but I was too relieved to be helping Henri to haggle.

I pictured my brother slaving on the ship, scrubbing decks and sleeping cold, and I shuddered. They would work him to death. His rescue could not be soon enough. And I could not count on help from my cousins, or from anyone else. It was only me. Who else had I ever been able to depend on?

Back in the shelter of the Roman folly, I switched clothing. I carefully rolled up the dress and wig and hid them in the shrubbery at the feet of the bronze angel in case I needed them a second time. I checked my reflection—boyish again —and strolled into the house.

Voices came from the direction of the foyer and stairs. I froze. It wouldn't do to run into company, especially if Treverton and his friend were still there. I doubted he would recognize me, but I needed this masquerade to last a little longer. And if Mrs. Medford saw me still in my dirty, old clothes, she would toss me out on my ear.

Looking for a servants' passage or a convenient hiding place, I tried one door that was locked and then another that swung open to the library. Thankfully, it was empty. The scent of leather book covers and paper welcomed me, and for a moment, I might have been home again.

But I had no time to mourn what was gone. I was supposed to be tutoring my cousins, and I felt a little guilty for taking the things from the attic, so this was a good time to start earning my board. I perused the shelves of books: histories, sermons—Anglican, of course—and a few novels. Probably either provided by the house's owner for the amusement of his tenants or left behind by previous holiday guests. If I was really trying to educate my cousins, I had little to work with.

The desk contained several sketchbooks, many with half-finished drawings. The artist had some skill, but she flitted from one subject to another without finishing her work. One of my cousins, no doubt. I shook my head. My father had made certain I could draw well—he often required me to sketch for him when he studied unusual plants or animals, and capturing every detail required patience and concentration. Drawing would be useful for my cousins.

The window looked out on the garden. It was as good a subject as any. I scrounged a few pencils and settled down to draw, quickly forgetting myself in the task. I'd left all my sketchbooks behind when we fled Paris, and it seemed like another lifetime when I had the luxury to sit and draw. Sketching had sometimes been a chore, a task required by Father, but now my pencil danced over the page, and I smiled. Father would have been pleased as I captured the details of the garden: the overgrown plants giving shelter to the quick sparrows foraging for autumn seeds among the fading flowers, the names of which I did not know in English. What had Father called them?

Father. My mind lurched back to France. Back to the guillotine. How could birds be singing here while blood flowed in France?

I ripped out my drawing of the garden with a vicious *shhhhck* and began another from memory. The human forms appeared only as a mass, because in truth, that's what they had been—a mob acting together without an individual thought. Individual thoughts were dangerous in a revolution. Above it all loomed the guillotine. And a dark stream swirled through the gutters and stained the feet of the jeering throng.

My breath came in tight bursts, and my pulse pounded in my throat.

"The library is this way!" a female voice called.

I gasped and blinked hard, trying to clear my head. My drawing of the guillotine swam before me. I touched the lines of the blade, my stomach churning.

Breathless giggles and the murmur of male voices drew closer. I tried to cover my sketch, my heartbeat still racing.

Frances bounced into the library, her face alight. I was glad to see company had cheered her, but I wished she had stayed away from the library. She pulled Treverton in behind her. He freed his hand to lift a quizzing glass and stare disdainfully at the paltry collection of books.

Loretta followed with Treverton's dark-haired friend.

"I must find that new novel," Frances said to Treverton. "I know you will want to read it because I liked it so. It was deliciously terrifying."

Her gaze fell on me, but she only gave me a vacant smile and skipped to the shelf to pull out a book.

She whirled back to Treverton. "Here it is! *The Mysteries of Udolpho.* Promise you will read it."

She raised the book to Treverton, forcing him to take it. He turned it over in his long fingers, his expression skeptical. "I will read it if it amuses me. I promise nothing more."

"I wish I could read it," a voice whispered behind me.

I started and looked around, but no one was near me, and none of the others seemed to have heard. Was I so lonely that my thoughts kept me company now?

Frances pouted at Lord Treverton, but her eyes sparkled. "I'm not frightened. I know you will love it because I do."

"We shall see," Treverton said. "But Hawke will no doubt read whatever the Miss Medfords ask him to." He cast a sly look at his friend.

Hawke had been staring around the library like he was looking for something. He gave a guilty start and pushed a strand of dark hair—sparsely powdered—from his face.

"Always happy to oblige a lady." Hawke flushed slightly and glanced at Loretta. His roaming gaze caught on my discarded garden sketch, and he scooped it up. "Ah, what's this? It must belong to one of you ladies. It's excellent, and I detect a feminine eye in its composition."

I froze. A feminine eye? Did male artists draw differently from female? I only knew how to draw what my father needed help with; my knowledge of artistic composition was limited. Would I give myself away so soon? Treverton gave me a speculative look, where I sat with a sketchbook in hand, and Hawke's attention turned to me as well. My mouth was so dry, I could form no defense.

But Frances looked from Hawke to me and snatched the drawing from him. "Oh, I do believe that's one of mine. Just a sketch. Nothing significant."

She lied so easily, I double-checked to be certain it was my picture. Loretta frowned at Frances. Did they guess I wasn't what I seemed?

"It's quite good," Hawke said. "Do you draw as well, Miss Loretta?"

"A little," she murmured. "Our cousin Charles is going to teach us more. Lord Treverton, Mr. Hawke, may I present Charles Cartier?"

Their gazes returned to me. I stood and bowed. "It is my humble pleasure."

Treverton's eyes narrowed. Did he remember me? Or see through my disguise? I tightened my grip on my sketchbook.

Treverton strode forward and tipped the sketchbook so he could see it, watching me the whole time. Only after meeting my eyes for a moment too long did he look down at the paper. His cold expression softened slightly as he took in my drawing of the guillotine.

He raised an eyebrow. "Young Mr.—Charles, is it?—will be an excellent teacher, I believe, as long as he restricts himself to scenes more appropriate for young females."

His voice sounded bored, but his words bore a trace of something—Amusement? Sympathy?—and he studied my face with curiosity. I lowered my eyes. Whatever he saw, I did not want to confirm his suspicions. I appreciated his warning—and that he did not speculate out loud on whatever he suspected—but I could not trust a man who tossed out gold coins one moment and sneered the next.

Treverton pushed the sketchbook back up so the girls wouldn't see it. I took a deep breath, trying not to flush. He made it seem as though I had drawn something scandalous. He didn't spare me another glance, though, and Frances once again took over the conversation. I sank back down into my seat, glad when the party left the room.

As soon as they were out of sight, I scurried upstairs for the safety of the attic. The quiet stillness of the space pressed around me, a crushing weight. I shut the door firmly behind me and poured out my coins to count them. Including the guinea from Treverton, I now had just over three pounds. And no expenses, since Mrs. Medford at least offered me shelter. I hadn't won my brother's freedom yet, but it no longer seemed impossible.

"It may come to more thievery, though," I whispered to myself.

"*Ooo, a scandal!*" said a voice over my shoulder.

Cold prickled over my skin. Who had overheard me? I

whipped around. No one else was in the attic, and the voice seemed to come at least half from inside my head. Had it been my own guilty conscience?

"Hello?" I asked, trying to make my voice sound deeper.

A long, tense silence filled the dimness.

"Hello?" The word came back like an echo, only in a very feminine voice.

"Is someone there?" I asked.

Someone was playing a trick on me, I was sure.

"Can you hear me?" the voice asked, rising a note in excitement.

Maybe it was a child. Maybe I could convince her that I had only been jesting about stealing. "I can hear you, but I can't see you. Where are you hiding?"

"Listen. Oh please, listen to my voice. Focus on trying to see me."

"What does that mean?" I asked, scanning the attic. "I don't even know where to look."

"Here. I am here in front of you. Say you can see me!"

I tried to track the sound and stared so hard my eyes ached.

And then a vague shape came into view, hovering just above the floor. I blinked hard to clear my eyes, but the figure was still there: a brown-haired young woman in a muslin dress. The same young woman I had seen in the window. *There* was a relative term, though, as I could see through her.

Impossible.

"What kind of trick is this?" I asked, mostly to myself.

"I wish it were a trick!" the young woman said, floating closer to me. *"I'm afraid that I am dead."*

I swallowed hard and took a step back, balling my fists so my fingers didn't tremble. "Ha! A ghost, I suppose. You must be one of the servants of the house, playing a jest."

"*A servant?*" the young woman gasped. Cold swirled through the room. "*Hardly! My family stayed in this house every autumn. They lingered for some time after I vanished last year, hoping to find what happened to me, but they never did. I thought once or twice my poor mama heard my voice, but it only made her cry more.*"

My heartbeat echoed in my ears. This could not be real. I was going mad. "And I'm supposed to believe I can see you when others cannot?"

"*I believe you have seen a great deal of sorrow. It opens your eyes. And you're not so self-involved as* some *people in this house,*" she added, folding her arms.

I could not deny I had seen sorrow. But I had never seen a ghost before. My father taught me to believe in the soul, but how had that ended for him? The Committee questioned him about his beliefs, if he supported the Church. In his absent-mindedness, he didn't grasp that the Revolutionaries wanted to sweep away all the ancient institutions and beliefs —and those who defended them. He told them his studies of the stars and the earth led him to believe a divine mind must have ordered the worlds. They had not liked that answer, nor the others that came after, and he never walked free again. In the Revolution, reason was supposed to supplant belief, but without belief, reason had turned to madness.

"I do not have time for madness," I mumbled, rubbing my eyes.

When I looked up again, the young woman was gone.

CHAPTER 5

I was seeing things. And no wonder. I was exhausted, distressed, and had hardly eaten for days. The scenes of the Revolution rolled through my mind waking or sleeping, colliding with guilt over Father and Henri. That was what haunted me, not some dead English girl in an attic.

It would do me good to find something to eat and not be left alone with my thoughts. Mrs. Medford begrudged me a single blanket, though, and she had been clear that I would not dine with the family. What if she allotted me only a daily crust of bread or bowl of gruel? My mouth watered at the thought of even such meager food. I couldn't help Henri if I fainted from hunger. I had to risk her wrath and find whatever sustenance I could.

The house had grown quiet again, the callers no doubt gone on their way, so I snuck downstairs to the kitchens.

A harried-looking woman stood at a table chopping carrots. Her knife hit the wood with a thunk that turned my stomach, and I squeezed my eyes shut, taking a deep breath. I was in England. No guillotines shaded the town squares here.

"What are you doing in my kitchen?" the woman snapped.

"I...uh...I think I'm supposed to eat down here?" It felt like begging again, which I had done my share of in recent months. I would almost rather steal. At least then I was taking control of my fate. "I can help you, too, if you'd like."

"You! Help?" She snapped the knife down. "You must be the fancy cousin from France. Well, I won't have no foreigners meddling with my kitchen. I suppose our food's not fine enough for you?"

I had to stifle a humorless chuckle. Whatever she thought of French cooks, her food had to be better than raw turnips scavenged from fields, but that was not the right thing to say.

"It smells delicious," I said. "I'm certain madam is an excellent cook."

She grunted. "There's some cold meat pie left in the cupboard. Eat that and stay out of my way."

My mouth watered at the thought. "Merci!"

I found the meat pie and dug in with an appetite sure to please a sensitive cook. The flaky crust and tender meat and vegetables practically dissolved in my mouth. I couldn't remember when I had eaten anything so delicious. My time before the guillotine was another life, like something I'd only read about in a novel.

"Mmm," I groaned in true appreciation.

She slowed her chopping and watched me curiously. "I'd forgotten what appetites young men have."

Ha! My starvation served me well if it helped my disguise.

"Is it true they put you in the attic?" she asked.

I nodded and took another bite.

She sniffed. "It's not a fit place for anyone."

I shrugged one shoulder and swallowed. "It's a place to sleep." I remembered what I'd seen...*thought* I'd seen up there. "Why is everyone so frightened of it?"

"Well..." She returned to her chopping. "Some of the maids heard strange noises. Had the door slam in their faces. One girl even swore something flew across the room at her."

My chewing slowed. The attic was drafty. No doubt that explained the disturbances. After all, no one else claimed to have seen a *person* up there. I swallowed a bite of pie, but it stuck in my throat, and I gulped some weak tea to wash it down.

After eating until I felt my stomach would split, I thanked the cook profusely and gathered my courage to head back for the attic.

All was quiet upstairs. A chill pervaded the attic, but we were near the sea with its cold winds. I sat heavily on the bed and wrapped the blanket around my shoulders. A few layers of petticoats would have kept me warmer. I rubbed my knees, the fabric of my trousers scratchy on my skin. I had not meant my boyish disguise to carry me so far, and when I thought of the scene in the library, I was certain it would soon crumble and reveal me. I did not know what the English expected from a gentleman. My foreignness might give me an excuse for some odd behaviors, especially among the ladies who were unlikely to have visited France, but it could not last.

I curled up on the bed with a tightness in my shoulders that would not unwind itself. If only I had someone on my side. Someone to help me. But who could I trust? I had to take care of myself, and also my brother. Just as I always did.

The exhaustion of the day finally dragged me toward sleep. As my eyes grew too heavy to keep open and I teetered on the edge of oblivion, I imagined a voice whispered, *"Good night."*

I woke with the dawn. Mrs. Medford would expect me to begin tutoring her girls, and to do it in cleaner clothes. With a weary sigh, I rose and sorted through the trunk of male clothes. I needed to alter them so they fit me better.

I stripped down to my stays, laced so they concealed my modest bosom.

"So, you are *a female!"*

I clutched a shirt to my chest and whipped around. The transparent young lady hovered behind me. My heartbeat thrummed, but surprise and anger overwhelmed all my other emotions.

"Am I not allowed some privacy?"

"I only thought you might want some help. You are not pretending very well."

"Shh!"

She shrugged. *"No one can hear me but you."*

I groaned and rubbed my eyes, but the young lady was still there when I looked up again. Perhaps I had gone mad, embracing a delusion fed by the cook's rumors. Perhaps...

perhaps some spirit had chosen me to torment because of my many deceptions. Either way, it might be a relief to talk to someone.

"Very well," I whispered, yanking the shirt over my head. "Yes, I am pretending to be a boy because I did not think Mrs. Medford would take in another female. They are my cousins, but I've never met them, and I was desperate for a place to stay."

The girl nodded. *"From what I have seen of her, I think you are right."*

"Then I chose correctly, only now I'm trapped in the farce."

The girl floated closer, her face brightening. *"I can help you. I can teach you to be a more believable gentleman."*

I stared at the transparent figure, the sense of unreality slowly settling around me until it began to feel comfortable, like a new gown. Or a new waistcoat. "Then I suppose you want something from me?"

"Mostly only someone to talk to. It has been so lonely this past year. It is very unfair to be struck down while one still feels so bright and anxious to see things in the world. You sound French. Are you French?"

"I am," I said cautiously.

"I seem to recall... there is trouble there?"

"There is."

"Oh, dear. I'm so very sorry. When I was alive, I didn't care much about such things, but now I know that I was a very selfish, silly sort of girl. I wish I could know more about the world now that it is too late."

"It might be better to have enjoyed your ignorance," I said.

"Oh, at the time, I did enjoy it very much. Only, I wish I knew how I died."

"A sickness?" I asked.

"Oh, no, it was something mysterious. My family never discovered what happened to me. Maybe an accident. Or a murder!"

"You talked to someone until they pushed you out a window." It was rude, and I should not have said it.

But the girl laughed. *"I do like to talk. I'm Beatrice Foley, by the way. I suppose we might use each other's Christian names in these circumstances. I know you go by Charles."*

"I'm Charlotte Carter," I said.

Beatrice drifted down as if she sat on the bed. *"Oh, very clever! Charles is easy to remember, then. But you must not have much practice at dressing as a boy, or I think you would know how to act the part better."*

"Of course I don't always dress as a boy! It was supposed to be only temporary." I did like how easy it was to move around, but the pants felt very thin on my legs. So very vulnerable.

"I wish I had thought to dress as a boy sometimes. I bet you learn a great deal. Maybe, if I had, I would have seen it coming."

"Seen it coming?"

"My death. I've had a great deal of time to think about it, and I suspect I was murdered. What I don't know is why or by whom."

Despite my jesting, I did have trouble imagining someone killing Beatrice. She seemed no different than any other charming but spoiled young lady of Society.

"Is there anyone you suspect?" I asked.

"I only remember that time vaguely. I'm afraid...afraid I am fading somewhat, and my memory with me. But there were dances. Parties. Handsome gentlemen."

"Hmm. Just because someone is a gentleman doesn't mean they couldn't hurt a young lady. Maybe one whose advances you rejected? Or you found out something to their disadvantage."

"Perhaps. I would like to know what had happened to me. At least so my mother could find my...my remains. And then, I think maybe I would be able to move on. Find peace."

I squeezed my eyes shut. I had to focus on Henri. I was all the help he had. But Beatrice needed my help, too, and no one else could see her. "I will see what I can do. But I have barely a month to save my brother. He is being held by smugglers over a debt."

"How exciting! Oh, I mean dreadful. I would help you there if I could."

"Maybe you will," I said, though I doubted she could do much for me or for Henri. "In the meantime, how can we help you?"

Beatrice bit her lip, an amusing gesture in a ghost. Then her face practically glowed. *"You will have to mingle with Society."*

"What!" I drew back. "Me?"

But Beatrice grinned. *"Yes! I will help you. I can teach you to be an English gentleman and an English lady. I know where there are some fine dresses in one of my old trunks. We will teach you the manners you need, and you can go to the parties. We'll see if we can find out anything about me."*

It was such a risky idea, I almost rejected it outright. But then I thought of the seven pounds I still needed to free Henri, and the days crumbling away while he wore himself out on the ship. If I did need to steal to free him, then Society was where I would find my victims. And, perhaps, mingling with wealthy people would give me opportunities to make money in more honest—or at least less dishonest—ways.

I nodded and picked up my needle to alter the boys' clothes. "Very well. We will help each other."

CHAPTER 6

"Enchantée," I said very carefully for the third time, emphasizing the soft sound of the "ch."

"En-chant-ay," Frances repeated, waving her fan with a bored expression. "I don't know why you keep repeating it. I'm saying it exactly as you do."

I sighed to myself. I did not actually care if Frances sounded like an idiot when she spoke French. After several days of trying to help her, I was nearly ready to write her off as a lost cause.

Loretta looked up from her French book. "But, cousin, you would say enchanté, would you not? Because you are male?"

I bit the inside of my cheek. That was the second time just that morning I had mistaken myself. "Of course, for me that is correct, but I am trying to teach you, and you are ladies."

Loretta looked satisfied and went back to her book. I rubbed my eyes. I was not going to survive this ruse.

"I think that's enough French for today," I said. "Work on your sketches, and I'll check back on you."

I needed to clear my head. I went out to the garden and sat on a bench, resting my face in my hands. This was all too much. But self-pity was a luxury I could not afford. I fumbled for the sketchbook shoved in my coat pocket and began a drawing of Lymouth, the low clouds from the sea hanging over the weather-beaten buildings.

"That's lovely."

I gave a start and found Beatrice hovering in front of me. The watery sunlight filtered through her form and washed out the details of her dress.

"I don't think I'll ever become used to you appearing like that," I said.

She folded her arms. *"I don't much care for it either. I can't control it all the time, and sometimes I just fade."* She shivered. *"But since you've arrived, I feel stronger. I think talking to you is making me more real."*

I had come to accept her as real, though a part of me still wondered if I was mad. I glanced around to be sure we were alone. "I'm glad to be helpful."

"And you like to sketch?"

I studied my drawing, smudging the shading on the clouds to give them a wilder and more menacing air. "I think it is one of the few areas where I have any accomplishment, along with languages. It allowed me to be useful to my father, and now to my brother and cousins."

She tilted her head. *"But do you enjoy it?"*

"I…" My fingers tightened on the pencil. No one had ever asked if I wanted to draw before. I had always done what needed to be done to keep Father happy and Henri well. Henri was only a child, after all, and Father… He was Father. "Why does it matter?"

She drifted in silent thought for a moment, then she sniffed. *"Well, any English lady—or gentleman—finds times for pleasure. It is what sets us apart from the working classes. Also, you are sitting incorrectly."*

I groaned and slammed my sketchbook closed. I could not even sit properly in England. "If I must mingle with Society, I would do best to stay in the background. Go unnoticed."

"Nonsense! I've heard the French excel at excess." Beatrice studied me with a frown *"But you are making yourself smaller like a female. You must sprawl. My brother always did. Men are the masters of their domain, after all."*

"I am not the master of anything."

"Well, neither are many of those men, but they still act like they are."

I couldn't argue with that. And Beatrice was probably as frustrated tutoring me as I was tutoring Frances. I sprawled out on the seat.

"Better. Now, use some of the cant I taught you."

"This bam is going to do me up," I grumbled.

"Oh, very good!" She laughed and clapped silently. *"You are going to bell the cat. Though, you also need to practice being a girl."*

"I am a girl!"

"I mean you should practice being a proper English lady.

There's a ball in a couple of nights..."

I shook my head. "I'm beginning to think that's not wise. I'm always on the verge of giving myself away. What if someone recognizes me?"

"That's why I'm teaching you. You'll be such a proper lady, no one will know it's you. You do know how to dance, don't you?"

"Of course!"

"Excellent. Then we will work on your bearing. You seem too anxious to please, and too bookish."

I was both of those things, but the way she said them, they didn't sound positive. "So, you want me to be boorish and stupid?"

She laughed. *"More like self-absorbed and witty."*

"Hmm." I thought I could manage to imitate that. I had been watching the Medford girls—Frances in particular— probably learning more from them than they learned from me. But going to a ball, dressed as a young lady, risked exposing me and getting me thrown out of the Medfords' house before I rescued Henri. "If I'm caught, I can't help my brother or you."

"You can't help anyone by hiding here, either."

I blew out a long breath and crossed my legs like a man. "But how will we make me look different enough?"

"There are so many things in those trunks. Wigs and patches. Even cosmetics. It will be very entertaining!"

It didn't entertain me—it made my throat feel dry and tight.

She saw my hesitation. *"I can go with you and help you think of ways to obtain extra money for your brother. Are you still thinking of robbing someone?"*

I sighed. "I don't want to steal."

"And I don't want to be trapped as a ghost. I think I'm becoming less solid, and I don't know what happens if I fade away completely."

"Maybe you go to heaven?"

"Or I stop existing altogether. There is darkness out there, on the edges, and it's creeping closer each day. It does not feel like heaven. Please. I'm frightened."

I met her terrified eyes, and my resolve collapsed. "Very well. Where are the cosmetics?"

That evening, we locked ourselves in the attic and went to work. Beatrice was right about the effects of a wig and some cosmetics. I worried that Treverton would remember me as a blonde, so I gave myself darker curls. I hesitated at the little face patches in a tin box.

"They're out of fashion."

"Try one!" Beatrice insisted. *"You'll be surprised how it changes you."*

I added a small round one on my cheek, where it drew attention to my lips painted with rouge. It made me look older—but that was a benefit. No one was likely to mistake this respectable, slightly old-fashioned lady for a French émigré boy. Between the two, I wasn't sure which was less like my real self. But at least I had my disguise.

CHAPTER 7

O n the night of the ball, I watched from my attic window as the Miss Medfords trooped outside with their mother to meet their hired carriage. Their pale gowns glowed in the twilight, and the tall feathers in their hair made them look like some unreal creatures from a fairy land. Indeed, the few times I had worn such delicate dresses seemed like a fairy story now. And even then, I had always felt a little out of place in such fine company, not as polished as the beautiful dancers in their slippers and wigs.

"Come, you must dress!" Beatrice motioned me over to the trunks.

"I'm not sure I should dress in the house."

"The garden is no place to ready yourself for a ball, and the Medfords are gone. Now, open the trunks."

I flung open the one she indicated. A pleasant scent wafted around me.

She inhaled deeply. *"It smells of lavender, doesn't it? Oh, I wish I could smell it. Or anything. Never mind, though. There's a white dress that should fit you well, especially when you release your bosom from its confines."*

I couldn't help laughing at that, despite the nervous flutters dancing in my stomach. I found a dress of fragile white fabric. "This one?"

"Yes, that will be splendid!"

I was afraid it would be ridiculous, especially since Beatrice had significantly more bosom than I did, even when mine was freed. But as I slipped on the undergarments and then wiggled the dress over my head, I found it surprisingly forgiving. Awkward to put on myself, but not impossible—thank goodness the newer fashions were much simpler, without hoops or tight waists. A little creative use of ribbon, and the dress fit well enough. I added the wig, patch, and rouge, and then turned to the mirror.

A haughty English lady stared back at me. Confident and witty. That's what Beatrice had said. I kept my chin up and tried to look the part.

The darkness had deepened outside. The ball would be well under way. I imagined the brilliant candlelight illuminating all those glittering people. Illuminating me. I flinched from the thought.

"We had better leave," I said. "Will you check to be sure the way is clear?"

Beatrice drifted out through the attic door, and I fidgeted with the dress while she was gone, admiring myself in the mirror. I didn't look so plain anymore. It wasn't something I had given much thought to in the past, but men might actually want to dance with me instead of hurrying past without a glance so they could consult Father...

Father was dead. I could not forget that. I was not going out to enjoy myself. I was going out to help Beatrice and my brother.

Beatrice reappeared. *"The main stairs are empty. Come quickly!"*

I whisked down the stairs from the attic to the main corridor. A door opened, and one of the maids stepped into the corridor. I turned my face and hurried for the next staircase. Perhaps the maid would not notice me. Or would not think anything odd about a strange lady walking about the house.

A shriek behind me shattered all such fantasies.

"Ghost!" a maid cried. "A white lady!"

I didn't look back but picked up my pace, nearly running to reach the stairs. No, another maid ascended with a basket of linen.

"There's an entrance to the servant's stairs in here," Beatrice called from one of the rooms.

I dropped the pretense of calm and jogged to the narrow doorway she indicated in one of the bedrooms, dashing through it and shutting it quietly behind me. I took only a moment to let my eyes adjust.

"She's vanished!" the maid called.

Perfect. Unless they remembered the servant's entrance. I scurried down the dark, narrow stairs as quietly as possible and stumbled out on the lower floor to rush for the garden. Staying low and keeping shrubbery between myself and the house, I managed my escape. The night air, tainted with the salty scent of the Channel, cooled my hot cheeks.

"That was a disaster," I mumbled.

Beatrice floated along beside me. *"No, they'll be so certain there's a ghost, they won't even think of you. Though, I suppose they're right about the ghost, even if it wasn't me they saw. I have tried to communicate with people in the house. Sometimes, if I concentrate very hard, I can move things, but that's all I've managed. I moved my trunk so you would see it that first day."*

"I thought it hadn't been there before."

"I only moved it a little, but it made you notice. I knew there was something different about you."

That was too accurate. This farce could not last. But I hurried in the direction of the ball, only forcing myself to slow when I drew close. A lady would not be rushing down the street. I shouldn't have even walked alone in this guise.

Carriages crowded the stone-paved street, and strains of stately music poured from the brightly lit house.

"How will I gain entrance?" I asked. "I don't know anyone there."

"I'll help you find a way in through the back."

Beatrice scouted out a path behind the house and directed me so I could appear to be reentering the house after stepping out for cool air. I took a deep breath of the fresh, green scent of the garden before approaching the back doors.

I straightened my dress and slipped into the ballroom. Crowds of young ladies and gentlemen danced, while jealous mamas watched from the sidelines. The Medfords would be here somewhere.

"Oh, this is a bad idea," I breathed.

"No, it's perfect!" Beatrice gushed. *"Think of the gossip you'll hear. And perhaps there's some way for you to acquire more money. You only have three weeks left to save your brother."*

I winced. No one else could hear her, but I didn't like hearing it aloud.

Beatrice guided me through the ballroom, telling me the right things to say to the right people. I greeted perfect strangers as she instructed and left a stream of confused people behind me. As we went, she told me of the guests she remembered.

"Miss Thorn over there was engaged last year, but she broke it off. Oh, there's Lady Blaine. She's a bore." She gasped and pointed. *"Oh, it's Lord Treverton! He always struck me as a villain."*

I glanced where she pointed, and his red-blond hair caught my eye. I could fancy the cold man who called on the Medfords as a murderer, but not the stranger who had given me a guinea. I needed to keep an open mind if I was going to help Beatrice find her answers, though.

I snapped my painted fan open to hide my mouth. "Do you think he killed you?"

Beatrice sighed. *"I'm not sure. I was quite taken with him. He is devilishly handsome, and the heir to an earldom. I often danced with him, and he called at my house a few times. He never did send me flowers, though."* She frowned over that. *"Everyone says he's wild—a rake! I know he's a shameless flirt. It was unwise of me to allow him to toy with my heart, but he is so amusing when it suits him to be."*

"Hmm."

Being a flirt didn't seem like a serious enough flaw to suspect him of killing anyone, but there was something a bit sinister about the way he surveyed the room, like King Louis before the guillotine brought him low. Girls tripped over themselves to catch his eye, and the mamas circled like vultures. He glanced my way, and I quickly raised my fan and looked the other direction. No need to risk being recognized.

"The card room is this way. You might overhear the men say something." Beatrice floated off to one side of the room, where an arched entrance led to another chamber.

A snuff box sat unattended on a side table, and I wondered what it was worth. I hated that my thoughts went to theft so quickly. I left the snuff box for now. It might be hard to sell without being caught, anyway.

I hesitated at getting too close to the card room. Alcohol fumes and raucous laughter poured out. *Cupshot*, I thought, remembering Beatrice's lesson in cant. No lady would go in that room. If I were dressed as Charles, I might have approached. Maybe even tried to win some money. But Henri's gambling was what had me in this mess.

I stationed myself as close as I dared to the card room, hoping to hear or see something useful to Henri or to Beatrice.

A man in a well-tailored evening suit stumbled out, shoving coins into his pocket. A shilling slipped through his fingers and rolled away from him, unnoticed. I shifted my foot to catch it. A very unladylike thing to do. I dragged my foot and inched closer to a chair where I might sit and fetch the coin. I shoved it in my slipper. It rubbed my foot but reminded me I was that much closer to saving my brother. This evening's risk hadn't been an entire waste.

Beatrice frowned at my antics but didn't say anything. Instead, she watched the well-dressed man stagger away from the card room. *"That's Lord Martin. A baron, but such a profligate. He sometimes danced with me, though he frightened me a little with his sharp tongue. It looks like he has fallen deeper into drinking."*

This was the second coin I owed to Lord Martin's drinking and gambling habits, then. Did such habits mean a man might also be a killer? He had known Beatrice, at the very least, and a man might drink to escape his guilt.

I watched the dancers from my seat. How thrilling it looked to spin about the room in a handsome man's arms, with no care in the world but that the music would end too soon. I watched wistfully for several minutes, then shook myself free of my daydreams. I couldn't afford them when people relied on me.

Frances and Loretta stood on the far side of the room. I snapped my fan open again to shield my face. Though my cousins lacked Treverton's knowing look, they saw me often enough that I might give myself away if I spoke to them.

But Beatrice turned in their direction, her eyes fixed on the man they flirted with—Lord Treverton's friend Hawke.

"Mr. Hawke is still single." Her tone lacked the excitement it held when she spoke of Treverton, but there was a wistfulness to it.

"You knew him?"

"He was courting me as well. He's not so thrilling as Treverton, but more likely to make a good husband. I might have chosen

him in the end. I think sometimes he was jealous of Treverton, and I felt so powerful when they both flirted with me." She sighed. *"But, of course, now I won't be choosing anyone, and he will marry someone else."*

I had no response to that. If Hawke had grown jealous of her flirting with Treverton and killed her, then he would have been a terrible husband. But if Hawke or Treverton had been jealous enough to kill her, it was strange that they were still friends.

Frances glanced my way. I kept my fan up, but she studied me with too much interest. I had the uncomfortable sense that others were looking my way as well. Perhaps realizing that I was a stranger.

"That's enough for tonight," I whispered to Beatrice.

I stood and hurried for the garden before she could protest. On my way, I nearly rammed into Lord Treverton again. Why was he always lurking nearby? He gave me a quizzical look, but I avoided his gaze and made a rushed—but feminine—exit.

CHAPTER 8

"*Wake up! Oh, you must wake up!*"

I started up in my lumpy bed. Beatrice hovered over me, her eyes wide with excitement.

"Is the house on fire?" I grumbled.

"*Of course not!*"

"Then why must you wake me?" I burrowed my face into the flat goose-feather pillow, but thoughts of the night before and the day ahead intruded on any chance of more rest. In addition to the ghost doing her best to shake me awake.

"*They will expect you up early. You were not supposed to have been out until midnight, you know. And there will be callers today. Gossip!*"

I groaned, but I couldn't deny any of what she said.

Putting my male clothing on again felt odd. I had to remind myself how to walk and talk like a young man on my way down the servants' stairs to the kitchen. Eating with only the harried cook was usually lonely, but it was for the best, since I might reveal my secrets if I spoke to anyone too much.

The cook paused from her work at the stove to plop a plate of toasted bread and strawberry preserves in front of me, along with a lukewarm cup of tea. It was a scant enough breakfast, and I wondered if Mrs. Medford ordered them not to feed me well. But it was more than Henri was likely eating on the smugglers' boat. I determined to devour every crumb on the plate and allowed myself the boyish luxury of licking a spot of sweet, sticky preserves from my finger.

One of the maids stomped into the room and tossed several pieces of broken pottery into a bucket. "She's done another one!"

The cook scowled. "What, another of the plates?"

"No, it's a bowl this time. Smashed it against the hearth."

I ate slowly, pretending not to listen. Was Beatrice practicing her haunting? No, I didn't think the maid would be so matter-of-fact about a ghost smashing crockery.

"That spoiled girl!" the cook said, shaking her head.

"The men didn't pay her enough attention at the ball last night," the maid said.

Would that be Frances? I couldn't imagine Loretta throwing anything, but Frances was... high-spirited. I hadn't believed her to be quite so temperamental. She was mourning her father, though, and no doubt under a great deal of pressure to marry well and help her family.

The cook flashed a quick look at me, and she and the maid grew quiet. I finished my breakfast and returned the plate. Then I made my way up to the library, hoping for a few more minutes of peace before I saw my cousin in a temper.

Mrs. Medford found me there as I organized the history books. She stroked the garnet necklace, her eyes distracted with worry.

"I'd like you to work with the girls on their sketching in the red drawing room," she told me. "Frances is overwrought this morning, and I think the sun there will do her good."

"Yes, madam," I said.

I fetched one of the sketchbooks from the desk and flipped through it. More flighty, half-finished drawings. Some of the drawings of people were good, though. I recognized quick sketches of Lord Treverton and Mr. Hawke, and there were a number of other men and women I didn't know.

I tucked the sketchbook under my arm and headed for the drawing room with its horrible, dark draperies. I was curious what the girls had to say about the ball.

Beatrice found me in the corridor and glanced at the sketchbook.

"Oh, what are we doing today?"

"Drawing lessons," I whispered, glancing over my shoulder. If anyone caught me talking to myself, they would think I was mad and throw me out.

"I wish I could sketch again!" Beatrice sighed. *"Being dead is quite dull. I'm certain I'm not meant to linger here."*

I felt for her. That was why I was trying to help her, after all.

Sunlight flooded the drawing room. The window opened on the street in front of the house, giving us a view of carriages transporting visitors to the beach. Loretta had already begun sketching, but Frances stared at her paper and pouted.

I glanced at Loretta's drawing of the houses across the street and nodded my approval. It was not fantastic, but it was passable. Frances had drawn nothing yet.

She gave me a defiant glare. "I am not in the mood to draw today."

"Sometimes drawing can be a good distraction from our worries."

"I tried it, and it doesn't work. Nothing can soothe me." She jutted her chin defiantly. There was something hard and sharp beneath her wilting exterior.

"*Gossip!*" Beatrice urged.

I sat across from Frances. Convincing my cousin to talk might help her as well as Beatrice. "Would you like to tell me about what's troubling you?"

She sniffed. "You don't really want to hear. You're only speaking to me because Mother told you to."

I wrinkled my forehead at her odd assumption, then I leaned forward and lowered my voice. "She wants me to teach you drawing, but if you would rather talk, I will listen. I want to help."

Frances sighed. "Oh, well, since you wish so much to hear about it, I hate to disoblige. Only, I am exhausted today. I danced all night last night, you see. Every dance."

That wasn't what I'd observed, but I could hardly say so. "That sounds entertaining."

"It made my feet ache. But of course, I can't say no. I don't want to disappoint my admirers. I know my obligations."

Beatrice rolled her eyes at that.

Frances fanned herself with her sketchbook. "I expect ever so many callers today, yet I am so weary."

"It is good to be well-liked," I offered, trying to find my way around her moods to soothe her.

Frances thumped the sketchbook against the arm of the chair. "There was a new woman at the ball last night. A mystery woman. Some of the men seemed very distracted by her. Not that I begrudge her the attention, of course. But men are so tiresome, dangling after one girl and then another. She didn't even dance with anyone, and she left before the dinner."

She shredded the edge of her pages, her lips curled down.

Beatrice tittered. *"She means you!"*

I stared at Frances, fighting the urge to laugh. How unkind of me. But was Frances really jealous? If only I could tell her I was not there to steal her beaus. And that one of them might be a killer.

The butler entered the room with a tray bearing calling cards.

Frances's wilting posture vanished, a hungry gleam in her eye as she snatched up the visitor's cards and grasped them like she was playing speculation and held the ace. "See them in."

I hadn't glimpsed the cards on the tray, but Beatrice said, *"It's Lord Treverton and Mr. Hawke."*

Oh, dear. I did not want them to see me again. Their eyes were too sharp. I retreated to the corner and took up my sketchbook, hiding behind it as I began a drawing of the girls.

The men entered the room, with Mrs. Medford trailing behind them like a hound hoping its master would drop a morsel of meat.

Treverton and Hawke bowed politely to the girls, who rose and returned curtsies. Beatrice was busy staring longingly at the two young men, leaving me uncertain what I was supposed to do. I remained hidden behind my sketchbook.

Mrs. Medford's eyes narrowed slightly when she saw me, but she could hardly complain that I was there when she had sent me to be with her daughters.

Treverton followed her gaze and studied me with interest, then shot an enquiring look at Mrs. Medford.

She put on a tight smile. "Lord Treverton, Mr. Hawke, I don't believe you have met our cousin, Charles Cartier. He is an émigré, recently fled the troubles, the only of his family to survive." She dropped her voice to a false whisper. "Aristocrats, you know."

Ha, now I knew where Frances found her tendency to exaggerate. But at least Mrs. Medford was unlikely to toss me to the streets if I made her look more important.

Beatrice motioned urgently for me to stand and bow, which I did.

"An aristocrat?" Treverton asked, a mocking lilt to his words as he looked over my newly mended clothes. His forehead wrinkled. "You know, I wonder if we have met."

Did I confess that first night in town and the guinea? I glanced at Beatrice for guidance, but she didn't know my dilemma and couldn't read my thoughts.

"Don't tell him you were at the ball!"

I had to bite my tongue to keep from telling her I wasn't an idiot.

Treverton turned to look where I was staring at Beatrice, and I quickly lowered my eyes.

"Course we met him," Hawke said. "We came upon him the other day in the library."

Treverton bowed his head in acknowledgment, but he still regarded me for a long moment before turning his attention to the girls.

The men paid me no mind after that, settling in to visit with the Miss Medfords and leaving me to draw in the corner.

"That's not polite, ignoring company," Beatrice warned me, but I still felt safer staying busy and out of the conversation.

After a few perfunctory remarks on the crush at the ball and the weather, Mr. Hawke turned his attention to Loretta's sketch.

"Oh, that is very well done, Miss Loretta."

She blushed and murmured her thanks.

Mr. Hawke turned his attention to Frances. "And have you been sketching this morning as well, Miss Medford?"

She waved a languid hand. "Oh, I am waiting for the right inspiration to strike. My mind is still a whirl from the ball last night. It was so delightful."

"Indeed," Mr. Hawke said. "I had a splendid time."

"It is unfortunate Lord Treverton is not so easily entertained," Mrs. Medford said. "I love to see young people dancing and enjoying themselves, but you scarcely danced at all, my lord."

"Perhaps he was distracted by the mystery woman," Frances said. "She was certainly intriguing."

Lord Treverton's lips curled in what was more a sneer than a smile. "She was playing games. She understands that it makes her more interesting."

"Interesting for an evening, certainly," Mrs. Medford said. "But a sensible gentleman prefers an honest girl. That's how I've raised my daughters."

Lord Treverton inclined his head but did not agree or disagree.

"Of course, Mrs. Medford," Hawke said quickly. "One cannot help admiring the modest and honest demeanor of the Miss Medfords."

My cousins smiled at that.

Beatrice rolled her eyes.

They fell into more dull topics of conversation. Treverton yawned and wandered over to see what I was doing. I resisted the impulse to hide my sketchbook since it would only make him more curious. I wouldn't try to seem mysterious for his amusement. I had sketched the entire party, though only in loose forms.

He nodded his approval of the drawing. "Did you have an opportunity to make the Grand Tour before the trouble started in France?"

I had rarely left France, but Beatrice nodded urgently.

"Yes, of course," I said, keeping my eyes on my paper.

"An artist would appreciate it, I suppose. What did you think of Venice?"

The others had stopped talking to hear my answer. My face warmed.

Venice. I added a bit of shading to my picture, trying to buy myself some time. What did I know of Venice? Canals. Botticelli. Or was that Florence?

"The canals—" I began uncertainly.

Beatrice made a face and pinched her nose.

"The canals stink," I said.

"What an unartistic view!" Mrs. Medford said. "I'm sure the canals of Venice are lovely."

I winced inwardly. Betraying myself again.

Lord Treverton smiled slightly. "No, your cousin is correct. The stench of the canals takes away greatly from the masterpieces of Venice. I much preferred Rome."

"You have traveled so much," Frances said. "I envy you."

"I am easily bored," Treverton said, not turning back to her.

"As am I!" Frances responded as if this were a positive trait to share. "Tell us more about your travels."

Treverton sighed and seated himself in an armchair, the grandest in the room. He began describing the various cities of the Grand Tour. Occasionally, he glanced at me as though we were sharing a jest. I tried to ignore him and focus on my sketch. Only when he began his description of Paris did I realize he was wildly exaggerating the things to be seen there. I shot him a scowl, and he smiled serenely.

Mrs. Medford exclaimed, "No, that cannot be true!"

"I'm certain your cousin will confirm my stories." Treverton glanced my way, something in his eyes I did not like. Was he testing me? Or perhaps he had seen through my disguise and was threatening me.

Beatrice circled him. *"He's lying, isn't he?"*

"Naturally," I said smoothly, answering her and Treverton at once. "Lord Treverton describes it exactly."

"I do not trust him!" Beatrice fixed her hands on her hips and stared him down.

I didn't trust him either. The Medford women gasped and cooed at his wild stories, and I kept my mouth shut, grateful when the polite time for a call ended and the men took their leave. More visitors came, and Beatrice recognized a few of them, but none made much impression, and it was only Lord Treverton I remembered by the time the morning calls were over and I could escape the drawing room.

"Did you hear?" Beatrice asked me.

"I heard a great deal of nonsense and nothing at all helpful."

"There is an assembly ball in a few days. There will be even more people there to question."

I groaned. I wanted to be done with attending balls and hounding after information. But I had gained an extra shilling for Henri from the last ball, and Beatrice needed my help, so I would attend.

A small, nasty voice in the back of my mind was amused by how disappointed Frances would be.

CHAPTER 9

Beatrice insisted on extra tutoring in the attic the afternoon before the assembly ball. Mrs. Medford had dismissed her girls early from French lessons, giving Beatrice plenty of time to walk me through the steps of every popular English country dance.

"They're going to hear me downstairs and wonder what I'm doing," I said when she instructed me on a scotch reel with its springing steps.

"*Oh, they are too busy fussing over feathers. No, wait! You're mixing up the steps of two dances.*"

"It's no use," I said. "I shall simply listen to gossip again."

"*Maybe we should find you one of those paper fans with the dance steps printed on them. Eventually, someone will ask you to dance. And once you've been properly introduced, it would be unthinkably rude to say no.*"

"What if I went as Charles?"

"*Your cousins would be horrified. Or, they would try to make you dance with other young ladies to keep Lord Treverton for themselves."*

"Yes, that would end badly. I don't know the men's parts at all." I flopped onto my bed. "Why does everyone dangle after Lord Treverton?"

Beatrice stared at me as though I'd asked why everyone needed to breathe. *"He's handsome, wealthy, and the heir to his grandfather's earldom."*

He was handsome, true, and clever as well—and he would never let anyone forget it. "I suppose after watching aristocrats fall to the guillotine, I find his anticipated title less impressive."

"You're the only person who's not impressed by Lord Treverton, then."

"The person most impressed by him is himself."

Beatrice laughed. *"No doubt true. He's had everything handed to him his entire life. He's come to expect it as his due."*

I wanted to say that I would never hand anything to him, but I remembered the knowing way he looked at me. He knew or guessed something about me, though I had no idea which of my many frauds he saw through. Someday, he might use that against me.

A pounding on the door made me jump to my feet.

"Charles!" Mrs. Medford called. "What is that racket up here?"

I winced and shot Beatrice a look. "I was just...moving some things around."

"Well, then you can come downstairs and help move furniture so the maids can clean. I want the red drawing room spotless before Lord Treverton calls next."

I groaned to myself. As long as my cousins were at Treverton's beck and call, I was as well. Now, I would be cleaning corners I doubted he would deign to turn his quizzing glass on.

The maid in the drawing room had already rolled up the carpet and pinned the curtains out of her way. I eyed the armchair warily, taking in its heavy wooden construction and unwieldy shape. Henri's work on the ship would be much more difficult than this. I steeled myself and grabbed one arm of the chair, trying to pretend it did not strain me to lift it. I considered sliding it, but I feared what Mrs. Medford would do if I scratched the floor.

The maid hmphed and grumbled to herself, "I don't know why they don't just 'ire a proper footman. Probably they like ordering around an aristocrat."

I wanted to argue that my cousins were likely short of funds after Mr. Medford's death, but I didn't need Beatrice to tell me that a gentleman did not argue with the staff about money.

The maid set her broom aside and took the other arm. I flushed at needing the help, but together we moved the chair and the rest of the furnishings to the center of the room. She covered them with dust clothes and gave the hearth rug a meaningful look.

I grunted and rolled the sooty thing up, then hefted it outside to the garden. Was I expected to beat it as well? It stained my hands and clothes with dark streaks. I tried to dust myself off, which only spread the grime. If I was cleaning, I would need an apron or smock of some kind, though that was certainly the type of thing a gentleman would never wear. I scrubbed my hands in the icy water of the bronze angel's shallow bowl, then went inside.

Frances admired herself in the mirror in the yellow sitting room. She caught my eye in the reflection as I passed and turned to the corridor with a too-bright smile.

"Oh, cousin, I hope you don't think me vain. I just don't want to disappoint Mother. But do you think Lord Treverton will admire my dress?"

I doubted he paid much attention to what ladies wore, but I said flatly, "I'm certain he'll think it's lovely."

She pouted for a moment. Then she stepped closer, her eyes wide and her lips parted slightly. "Do *you* admire my dress, cousin?"

The way she spoke sent a crawly shiver over my skin, as though she was trying to worm her way into some shared secret with me. Was she threatening me—implying that I was female and wanted to wear the dress? Or—heaven forfend—was she flirting with me?

I took a step back, farther into the safety of the corridor. "I know little of English fashion."

She laughed, a tinkling sound full of sharp, brittle edges, and motioned to my sooty clothes. "That is clear enough." She smirked and leaned closer as though sharing a confidence, though her words came out cold. "If you learned to be less careless with yourself, Mama might not be too ashamed to let you go out with us. I can't imagine how lonely it would be, to be stuck in the house all day with no one who wishes to acknowledge you. I want to help you, but I wouldn't know where to begin."

The words cut, exposing my utter aloneness. And from

the gleam in her eyes, they were meant to. I hadn't seen such joy in cruelty since the mobs of France, and I caught my breath, tempted to flee the house.

But I had nowhere else to run. I had to survive, and I had to do it here.

Frances spun back to the mirror to preen, her cheeks glowing. "I only hope I am lovely enough to be countess as Mama wishes. Am I as pretty as a French comtesse?"

There was no sincerity in the question, but I sensed it would be dangerous not to play her game. I shut my eyes, and scenes of bloodshed painted my vision red. "The last comtesse I saw was Madam du Barry. They cut off her hair and led her crying for mercy to the guillotine, where they sliced off her head. I would say you have some definite advantages over her."

Frances frowned. "You are trying to be droll, but you forget: My father is dead. I do not enjoy such humor."

I stared as she turned back to her preening, her face serious. Could she not understand anything beyond the reach of her own fingertips? But perhaps her pain engulfed her so that she could not see beyond it. Perhaps she tried to ease her hurt by pushing it on others.

Mrs. Medford swept past me, sparing a disdainful look for my dirty clothes, and stood beside her eldest daughter. Loretta, trailing in her mother's shadow, stopped beside me, blocking my escape.

"You look marvelous, my dear." Mrs. Medford beamed at Frances.

Frances dimpled. "I do hate to put myself forward, but I know my duty. And I will make Lord Martin regret his unkind words when he sees me dancing with Lord Treverton!"

"Now, dearest," Mrs. Medford said. "They both have their...youthful follies, but either would be acceptable for you girls. Though, Lord Martin is only a baron. Lord Treverton will be an earl when his grandfather dies. And we have an advantage with him since his grandfather looks favorably on our family."

Loretta rubbed her forehead and said nothing. I thought she looked paler than usual, but she put on a stoic face.

"Perhaps I should wear some fetching jewelry," Frances said, frowning at her reflection. "Pearls. Or even a jewel. Everyone crowds Lord Treverton, and it would be unfair if he accidentally overlooked me in the press."

Mrs. Medford's hand went to her throat. Her garnet necklace was gone. Her lips tightened, deepening the worried lines around her mouth and eyes. "Such jewelry would not be seemly."

Frances pouted.

I watched Mrs. Medford from the corner of my eye. All these dresses must have been expensive. Was she selling her jewelry to pay for them? A stab of guilt shot through me for being so critical of my cousins. They were struggling.

"A different hairstyle then," Frances said. "Something to catch his eye."

"That might be wise," Mrs. Medford said. "I've heard from several sources that Treverton's grandfather is pressuring him to choose a bride at last. It's not an opportunity to be missed."

Frances giggled, but then her face fell. "Oh, but then, I really do need to change my hair. More feathers!"

"We will be very late," Loretta said, almost too low for anyone to hear.

"You can keep your beaus waiting as well as I can!" Frances said, hurrying back upstairs.

Loretta watched her go with a forlorn expression.

"I'm sure any young man would be happy to see you whenever you arrive," I told my cousin.

She smiled sadly. "You always know just what to say. You must have had a sister."

Mrs. Medford gave me a suspicious look. She probably thought I was forming designs on her daughter.

"I hope you enjoy the ball tonight," I said quickly and retreated to the safety of the attic until they left.

CHAPTER 10

Finally, Frances must have been satisfied with the number of feathers in her headpiece. A hired carriage grumbled its way down the dark street, its lantern swaying as it carried my cousins toward the assembly hall.

"Time to leave," I told Beatrice.

I had learned from the first ball. I would not dress in the house and sneak outside. It was too risky. Instead, over Beatrice's protests, I bundled up my clothes and walked out to the garden folly.

"You can't change out here!" Beatrice hissed, looking around the dark shrubbery.

"You can make certain the way is clear, but this is much less risky than walking through the house dressed as a woman."

"How will you know that you look well enough?"

"You'll have to tell me," I said and proceeded to strip down in the shadows of the Roman folly.

Dressed as a lady once more, I checked my cosmetics in the reflection of the bronze angel's shallow basin. The moon was nearly full, giving me welcome light, but reminding me that Henri's time was slipping away.

Beatrice fretted, but in the end, she admitted that I looked passable.

"Are you going to talk to Hawke tonight?" she asked.

"About you? I'll try."

"And Lord Treverton?"

"I'd rather not." He saw too much. Maybe knew too much.

"But he might have killed me, don't you think?"

I thought about how his eyes changed, sometimes amused, sometimes indifferent. "I don't know. I have seen mobs kill people, but I don't know what would make an individual do it."

Beatrice floated along with me as we approached the assembly rooms. This time, I could enter through the front doors, though it cost me a few precious coins. I didn't know if there would be much card playing here or if some unlucky gentleman would drop more coins. If I saw an opportunity to gain a few shillings, though, I would have to take it.

The assembly rooms looked out over the sea, and for a moment, all I could think was that my brother was out there somewhere, suffering alone.

Beatrice's lessons were paying off, though. I was not quite so frightened to be seen at this assembly, and I felt more certain of my disguise. I caught Frances watching me again, but I pretended not to notice. Hopefully, she saw me as a rival, not as her cousin.

I scanned the crowds, looking for our suspects. Lord Martin leaned against a wall, his eyes already glassy from drink as he frowned vacantly at a hopeful mama encouraging him to dance with her daughter. Lord Treverton stood amid a swarm of young ladies, his expression utterly bored.

"Mr. Hawke is not here." Beatrice sounded as disappointed as if she had expected to dance with him herself.

I shook my head. I did not see him either.

"You must speak to Lord Treverton, then," Beatrice reminded me. *"If he is not guilty, he probably knows the person who is."*

I groaned inwardly, but she was right. I needed information, and he likely had at least some.

"It will be difficult to draw him away from all those ladies," I said under my breath.

"You have to flirt with him like I taught you," Beatrice prompted. *"I was very good at flirting when I was alive."*

I felt absolutely foolish, but I strolled near Lord Treverton, making certain that he saw me. I made brief eye contact, then looked away as if bored.

"Now drop your fan," Beatrice prompted.

I was likely to never get it back in that crowd, but I did as she said and let it slide from my fingers as I continued walking.

"Don't look back."

Halfway across the room, I began to wonder if Beatrice had miscalculated my approach. But no, a man's footsteps followed me.

"Pardon me, miss," Lord Treverton said.

I turned to stare up into his green eyes.

"Yes?" I asked coolly, trying to sound as English as possible.

His lips quirked on one side. It was a game, and he knew it. "We have not been properly introduced, but I believe you dropped this."

I softened my expression and gasped. "Oh, my favorite fan!" I smiled. "I suppose I can forgive the improper introduction since you've done me such a kind favor."

The word improper rolled off my tongue with a lilt.

He raised an eyebrow. "You are not English."

"I had a French nursemaid," I replied. True enough.

"Really?" he asked, studying my face again. "How...interesting."

I didn't flinch from his curious gaze. Was he comparing me to the Medford's male cousin? Why should he? I looked nothing like myself.

"And do you dance?" he asked.

"Remember—witty and mysterious!" Beatrice said.

As if it were that easy. I put on a bored expression. "With the right partner."

"Who might be such a lucky partner?"

"He would have to be both interesting and kind."

"Interesting and kind. A difficult combination. For interesting people are often self-absorbed."

"Are they?" I asked. "How unfortunate. But perhaps because you do not meet the qualifications, you think no one else can."

He put a hand up to his chest in mock offense. "I thought we already determined I am kind."

I grinned at him. "So we did. *Kind.*"

His eyes widened, and he laughed. The sound rolled through me and filled me with a pleasant warmth.

He extended a hand. "May I have the chance, then, to prove that I am also *interesting*?"

"Only because you returned my favorite fan."

"Ah, I'm a charity case, then?"

"Oh, not at all. If you fail to entertain me, you will owe me something."

He bowed. "I will take that risk."

He led me out to the floor, and we joined a set of dancers. I felt many eyes watching me, no doubt Frances's among them. I hoped I was not overstepping the bounds of my luck.

"Now," he said as the movements of the dance brought us together. "I cannot speak of the roads or the weather. Much too dull. How shall I demonstrate my conversational skills?"

"Tell me about the town. Not the weather or the roads, of course. I would like to know more about Lymouth."

"Ah, there I can shine, for Lymouth is an interesting town." He pulled me a little closer as we met in the middle of the set. He smelled like orange water, sharp but pleasant. "It is a smugglers' den, you know."

"Is it?" I feigned surprise. "Does that make it dangerous?"

"Not to us as we dance here, but out in the streets at night, it would be dangerous to see the wrong thing."

We wove our way around the outside of the other dancers and came together again, our steps matched. Beatrice's lessons were paying dividends.

"What sorts of things should I avoid seeing?" I asked.

"Faces, for certain. You should never see faces. If you

notice any strange activity, turn your eyes to the wall. If you can say you have seen nothing, you will be safe from the revenue men and the smugglers."

"Ah, and if this is well known, then I'm sure no disasters befall innocent young ladies."

His forehead wrinkled. "Normally, I would say there is little danger to your person. But there was a great mystery last fall. A young lady vanished as if into thin air."

My breath caught. Could it be this easy? "Surely, she eloped with a secret lover."

"I thought as much as well," Treverton said, lowering his voice and bending near so his breath tickled my ear. "But she never reappeared, married or not. No, I have since wondered if she knew something dangerous."

"Hmm." I forced myself not to be distracted by his warmth, his nearness. Was this only idle gossip, or was he warning me? Or baiting me?

The steps of the dance separated and then reunited us.

"Well?" he asked.

"Well?" I responded.

"Are you now convinced that I am interesting?"

I needed more information from him. I cocked my head. "I think you are an entertaining storyteller, but this sounds too fantastical. I do not know if I believe your story."

He waved a hand. "It's well-known gossip around town. I'm sure you can find someone to verify it."

"Then it won't be interesting, because everyone knows it."

He narrowed his eyes. "Is it secrets you're after? Those can be dangerous."

"Are you threatening me now? That is neither interesting nor kind."

"But warning you is both, my dear. You have your own secrets. I find them intriguing. Just as I find you intriguing." He pulled me near again—nearer than the dance required—his gaze brushing my face and making my cheeks warm.

The steps of the dance pulled us apart, and when we drew together again, he was smiling, self-satisfied.

"There," he said with a smirk. "Now I have proven myself interesting, have I not?"

I stared at him in astonishment, nearly missing the next turn in the dance. Had he truly been warning me, or was he only playing the game with me still?

Beatrice signaled to me. Frances had managed to maneuver herself and her partner into the same set as us, and she was working her way up the line of dancers. Soon, we would be face-to-face.

I dropped Treverton's hand and backed away, heedless of the other dancers. "I must have fresh air."

"But—"

I turned and fled into the crowd, wishing I could vanish as easily as Beatrice. If Treverton was dangerous, I didn't want him to think any more of me, though I had trouble making myself stop thinking of him. The scent of orange water lingered on my gloves.

"You flirt very well!" Beatrice said, catching up with me outside. *"He watched you go and looked quite sorrowful to see your departure."*

"He spoke of secrets and danger," I breathed to her. "Is he your killer, though?"

"I'm still not certain. Oh! He has come to the door. He's looking for you!"

I refused to look back. Instead, I picked up my pace and dodged my way down an alley. As far as Treverton or anyone else at the ball was concerned, I had vanished into the night.

CHAPTER 11

My antics at the ball drew more than Treverton's attention. The next day, Mrs. Medford summoned me to help soothe my cousins' nerves. Loretta retreated to the ballroom to practice a sad song on her pianoforte, but Frances paced the drawing room with a frantic energy only broken when the butler entered bearing calling cards.

I tried to slink off for the library, but a gaggle of girls swept into the room, blocking my escape. I remembered to bow, and Frances gave me a speculative look.

"Ladies," she said, rattling off their names, "I must introduce you to my cousin, Charles Cartier, an aristocrat recently escaped from the guillotine."

They oohed and aahed over me like a monkey in a cage.

"How did you escape?" one girl asked, sizing me up in a way that made me feel very uncomfortable.

"Uh..." I tried to think of how to frame my story.

No need. Frances jumped in with a gothic tale of deception and misfortune that put *The Mysteries of Udolpho* to shame. The girls all stared at me with awe, and I fought the urge to hide my face.

Beatrice drifted into the room as Frances detailed a heart-wrenching scene where I sobbed over a jewel entrusted to me by Marie Antoinette on her way to the guillotine and then used it to bribe an innocent maiden's way out of prison.

Beatrice laughed. *"Now I know why my brother warned me not to read so many novels."*

"I wonder if the mystery lady last night was also an aristocrat," one of the young ladies said. "I've heard she's French."

Frances's eyes narrowed slightly, then her features smoothed, and she shrugged one shoulder. "I prefer not to speculate about someone so crass."

"Oh, her manners were terrible—clearly foreign—but she was beautiful, didn't you think? And Lord Treverton certainly seemed taken with her," another girl cooed.

"The way she flirted!" The third young lady shuddered.

With that, they quickly eviscerated every aspect of my behavior the night before, then speculated about my identity. I could only stand there and simmer in my foolishness. I should never have undertaken this deception.

Frances put on an air of derision when discussing me, but once her guests left, she sank onto the sofa and pounded it with her fists. Then she burst into tears. "How can I compete with someone who has the entire town talking? Our entire trip to Lymouth will be wasted."

Beatrice hmphed at Frances. *"At least you have not been murdered—yet."*

Guilt twisted in my chest. I was not trying to ruin my cousins' chances or their happiness in Lymouth. "Certainly, it's not a waste if the seaside brings you comfort."

"Oh, what would you know of it?" Frances said between sniffles. "You don't understand what it's like to have poverty hanging over your head—your entire family's fortune resting on your shoulders."

I stared at her in disbelief.

Mrs. Medford came into the room with Loretta hanging in her shadow.

"What are you saying that upsets Frances?" Mrs. Medford snapped at me.

"Just speaking of the mystery lady like everyone else," Frances grumbled.

Mrs. Medford petted Frances's hair. "Don't fret. The men might flirt with such a woman, but none would want to marry her."

My face warmed at that. I wasn't hunting a husband, but of course, she was right. After this masquerade, no decent man would want me.

Frances dabbed her eyes on her mother's handkerchief. "Yes, she's probably some common adventuress mingling with decent people. I'm sure such things are not tolerated in France, are they cousin?"

"No, they are not." Before the Revolution, kings and lords openly flaunted their common-born mistresses, and I had felt sorry for their wives. But now, nothing was tolerated in France.

The butler returned bearing calling cards.

Beatrice peeked at the tray. *"Treverton and Hawke are here! Now you can hear something useful!"*

My chest tightened, and I looked for an excuse to flee. I could not risk Treverton remembering my face.

But their footfalls approached too quickly over the soft carpets. I was trapped. I took up my sketchbook and huddled in the corner, losing myself in a drawing of the University of Paris when scholars still filled its halls.

After the usual greetings, the men settled into chairs, Treverton again taking the finest.

"We missed you at the ball," Loretta said quietly to Hawke.

He looked uncomfortable. "I found myself...unable to attend, but I am sorry to have disappointed you."

"Interesting," Beatrice muttered.

"And you enjoyed the ball?" Mrs. Medford asked Treverton.

Mr. Hawke smiled. "He must have. I hear he had the opportunity to dance with the mystery lady. He won't tell me anything about her, though."

"She speaks with a French accent," Treverton said.

I froze. I could feel his eyes on me. I couldn't resist. It was too strange if I didn't respond to that, so I looked up. Everyone was staring at me.

"Do you by chance have a sister?" Treverton asked.

Loretta looked at me as well.

My mouth went dry. I was caught. I hated to dig deeper into my lies, so I danced with the truth. "I have one sibling, monsieur," I said, wrapping my words securely in my French accent. "But not here in England."

"There are many French people here now," Frances said with a dismissive wave. "And some people might think it alluring to pretend to be French. I want to hear some real news. Certainly, something more interesting is happening than the gossip from a ball."

"Oh, yes!" Treverton said. "There was a fight last night between the militia and some smugglers."

Beatrice gasped and looked at me.

My chest squeezed. Not Henri! But no, his smugglers would be back at the next new moon. We still had a little over two weeks.

"Smugglers?" Frances asked. "That is exciting."

"Really, Frances," Mrs. Medford said. "I hope they caught the criminals!"

"Not this time," Treverton said. "But they will."

"What do they do with smugglers when they catch them?" Frances asked.

"They hang them, of course," Treverton said.

The conversation meandered on through discussions of smuggling, France, and an upcoming masked ball. None of it mattered to me. My brother could be caught and hung. My fingers shook so I could not draw. I had to save him from those smugglers.

As soon as the men left, I mumbled an excuse and fled the room.

"*There is to be a masked ball,*" Beatrice said, her eyes bright.

"So I heard." The last ball had not been very helpful in getting answers, and I was still afraid I would be found out. "I can't... I can't go to another ball. I have to get the money I need to save my brother. You heard what they do to smugglers."

"Oh, I'm sorry! How thoughtless I am." Beatrice considered. *"There's more you can sell in the attic. Some of my old things. I certainly don't need them, and they must have been too painful for Mother to keep. I will help you look."*

"Thank you," I said.

"One of the trunks has a fine shawl and gloves with beadwork. Those should be valuable, and I think my red dress..." Beatrice stopped and hovered in place. *"It was a masked ball."*

"Yes, I heard."

"No, I mean, the last night that I remember. The night I died."

"You died at a masked ball? It seems crass to hold another."

"I didn't die at the ball. I don't think. But bits of it are coming back to me. My last night. The costumes." She stared absently, then bit her lip. *"If there's another masked ball, perhaps people will speak about me."*

I sighed but looked on her with sympathy. "I don't think a murderer would take the opportunity of a masked ball to confess his misdeeds."

"Ah, but there's one thing you're not considering."

"What's that?"

"You could go dressed as me."

"As you? We are not much alike."

"But the costume I wore to last season's masked ball is still in the attic. It was very memorable. Imagine how shocked everyone

would be if you appeared looking exactly the same. It might push someone into slipping up. Or remembering something."

I chewed my lower lip. I hated the idea, but she could be right. "Just how memorable is this costume?"

"Come see!"

I followed her to the attic, and she directed me to a small trunk I had overlooked.

"This one." She pointed. *"They packed it away last."*

I took a deep breath of the stale, dusty air and opened the lid of the trunk. On top of the clothes inside sat a mask topped with bright red feathers.

"What is it meant to be?" I asked.

"Look at the rest of it," Beatrice urged.

I found a red gown and a cloak decorated with red and blue feathers to match the mask. It was entirely too garish for my tastes, but I had to admit it was stunning. And difficult to forget.

"A parrot?" I asked.

Beatrice nodded enthusiastically. *"Isn't it lovely? I saw one in a cage, and I thought it was so clever and pretty, I had to have it as a costume. I liked it better than the canaries because it didn't have to stay in its cage all the time."*

"Hmm." I held up the dress. It would fit me, and it would certainly stand out.

"There are slippers, too."

"Oh, I think I remember them! They were in one of the other trunks."

I rummaged carefully through the delicate gowns until I found the slippers with their red feathers. That was almost too much. But it would certainly draw attention. Maybe even attention from Beatrice's killer.

"Oh," I said, setting down the slippers.

"I know it's a great deal of red, but I think you'll look fetching in it."

"It's not that. If someone did kill you, how will they react if they think you're still alive?"

"They'll think you're a ghost. Maybe it will frighten them into giving themselves away."

"Or, if they aren't sure they killed you the first time, they might try again."

Beatrice's eyes widened. *"I see. I suppose no one knows where the rest of me is. My body, I mean. The killer might have buried me, but if he pushed me off a cliff or into the sea, he might doubt that he was successful."*

We stared at each other.

"I'm sorry," I said. "This must be a painful conversation."

"It's not pleasant, but I've spent the last year thinking it over. It's actually comforting to be able to talk about it."

However lonely I had been, how much worse was it for Beatrice? And someone owed her justice. I hated the thought of a killer walking free—a killer who had struck down one young lady and might claim more innocent lives. I could not stop the relentless rise and fall of the guillotine blade, but maybe I could stop bloodshed here.

"Very well." I took a deep breath and stared at the red scattered all around me on the floor. "I will wear the costume to the ball. You will come with me to watch how people react and to tell me if anyone seems likely to hurt me. I'll wear my trousers and shirt under the costume so I can change quickly if needed."

Beatrice nodded, her eyes wide. *"I will watch over you."*

I wished she could do more than watch, but it would be up to me to take care of myself.

Her eyes brightened. *"And I'll search the rest of this house and see if my family left anything behind that you can sell to help your brother."*

"Really?" I asked.

"Of course. I'm sure my family took the things that had sentimental value, and I don't want Frances Medford to have anything of mine."

I considered that. My cousins lived with a thin purse, and I didn't want to take from them, but if anything in the house belonged to Beatrice, she could dispose of it as she pleased.

"Thank you," I said.

I wanted to help Beatrice either way, but knowing we were getting that much closer to saving my brother doubled my resolve to help her find her killer.

CHAPTER 12

I could not escape the gossip about the mystery woman. About me. The Medfords' visitors brought it into the house like dust on their shoes, the maids spread it around as they scrubbed together in the kitchen and hung laundry alongside neighboring maids, and when I snuck out to sell the things Beatrice directed me to, it whirled around me in a storm.

"She's a *princesse* escaped from the guillotine."

"No, a French heiress with pillows stuffed full of diamonds."

"Nothing but a common adventuress pretending to be French."

"A French spy! We should turn her in to the militia."

Beatrice, hovering beside me in the secondhand shop, listened to all of it with wide eyes.

"I never imagined we would stir such interest! Just think what

will happen when you show up at the masquerade in my costume!"

I groaned inwardly. Probably, I would be mobbed by people either looking for my supposed jewels or trying to arrest me. My only consolation was that I would be dressed as Beatrice, and it was unlikely that anyone would connect her with Charles.

Beatrice gasped, snapping me out of my thoughts.

She gestured at the woman behind the counter. *"She's trying to take advantage of us. Those gloves are worth a shilling more than that at least!"*

I forced myself to focus on the transaction, and I walked out of the shop two pounds closer to Henri's freedom.

Beatrice spun in the street, passing through at least one pedestrian. *"We have more than half of it now, and still almost two weeks until the next new moon!"*

I smiled at her use of "we." I'd never had anyone who felt like a partner before. Mother made me feel that way when I was young, though of course I could never manage as well as she had. As proven when she died and I was left to muddle through on my own. Then I lost father as well. And Henri. Guilt swam in my belly. If only I could find answers for Beatrice.

I had gone to the shop as Charles, so I didn't need to change clothes this time. I still entered through the garden. The Medfords couldn't discover I had been selling Beatrice's items; they certainly would not understand. As much as I wanted to help them, I could not let them have Henri's money.

But Mrs. Medford caught me coming in through the

back. "What have you been doing outside while the rest of us are working to prepare for the ball?"

I shoved my hands into my pockets to hide my coins. "Just enjoying the fresh air."

"Hmm. Since you like spending time in the garden, you can clean it up. We don't want anyone to get a bad impression of us."

Frances wailed something from upstairs, and Mrs. Medford left me.

"They wouldn't want anyone to get the right impression of them." Beatrice glared after Mrs. Medford.

I slunk back outside before answering. "I owe them something for my room and board."

"As if watching those girls butcher your language and draw poorly isn't enough. Do you actually want to help them?"

"I don't know. I don't like to see them suffer, and...and this is what I've always done. Since my mother died..." I trailed off. "The problems always fell to me, and I dealt with them."

"I don't think I ever thought about much besides myself. You must be strong to always carry the burdens of others."

Was I strong? I never felt I had a choice. I shrugged and studied the gardens. I didn't want to expose my Roman temple more, but I could trim the hedges close to the house. I'd never cut hedges before, but I turned up some rusted clippers. I would manage.

The hedges might have disagreed. Between the dullness of the clippers and my inexperience, the poor things looked rather ragged from my efforts. Maybe I was not helping my cousins much after all. Their voices drifted from the window as they prepared their costumes for the ball that night. I thought of the parrot costume in the attic with a mix of dread and—surprisingly—excitement.

"Charles!" Mrs. Medford called. "Oh, the French are so lazy. Charles!"

I grumbled to myself but set the clippers aside. The rest of the shrubberies were safe for the moment. I followed Mrs. Medford's voice upstairs to find Loretta and Frances in their white dresses.

"Oh, there you are," Mrs. Medford said, exasperated. "We need to remove a chair from Frances's room. Frances has spilled her wine—"

"My maid startled me," Frances said, a storm brewing in her eyes. "It ought to come out of her pay."

"Yes, dear," Mrs. Medford said quickly. "Of course, I mean that the maid spilled your wine. It has stained the upholstery."

"A little wine splashed on my slippers, too," Frances hissed. "They are supposed to be white, but now they have a pink spot. I can't wear them like this. I'll look slatternly!"

"Maybe there are other slippers in the attic," Mrs. Medford said. "I've been meaning to go through the trunks up there."

"Don't let them see my costume!"

I looked at the stains and the poor maid's expression. "I can remove the stains, and the slippers and chair will be like new."

They all stared at me.

"Men don't clean fabric!" Beatrice gasped.

Frances's eyes narrowed. "What odd things they teach young men in France."

I flushed. "Because my mother died early, and my father was often distracted, I sometimes had to oversee the housework."

"Then you'd best work quickly," Mrs. Medford said.

"I wonder if you would rather be cleaning than dancing." Frances watched me with a malicious gleam in her eyes. "Don't you wish you could go to the ball?"

I shook my head. "No, thank you. After Paris, crowds do not appeal to me."

I lifted the chair with the slippers on top, careful to make it look easy so they would think me strong and male, and hurried out of the room.

"She suspects something," Beatrice warned.

I nodded, not daring to speak. I didn't know if Frances saw me for a girl, but she was suspicious of my story.

I hurried down to the kitchen for some boiling water to treat the slippers. The cook gave me a strange look when I showed her what I needed to do. Then she shook her head.

"It's like them to have their own flesh and blood doing such tasks."

"I don't mind helping," I said, feeling like I needed to defend myself.

The cook watched as I worked on the stain. "There now, you've done this before."

"My father was careless. I saved many a cravat from being discarded with this trick."

"You'd make an excellent lady's maid," the cook said.

I froze and glanced up at her, trying to look confused instead of terrified.

"If you were a girl," she added.

Then she turned back to her stove.

I swallowed hard. She knew. She had no reason to expose me—yet—but how many other people would see through my disguise? I was eating better, and my thin frame filled out a bit more each day. It was good that I would be leaving as soon as Henri was free or everyone would know my secret.

I returned the spotless and slightly damp slippers to Frances, who took them without a word of thanks.

Then I hurried back to the kitchen to blot the chair, keeping a watch on the sunset. I had the fabric clean by the time I heard the carriage jangle up to the front door. I peeked out the window to be sure my cousins were really leaving.

Dressed as Greek goddesses, their long white gowns glowed and paste jewels sparkled in their dark hair. Their small masks covered only a sliver of their pretty faces. They giggled in nervous excitement as the driver helped them into the carriage.

I envied them for a moment as they rode off, able to enter the front doors of the ballroom as themselves. Not afraid of being unmasked as frauds.

Once the carriage rolled out of sight, I bundled up the parrot costume and snuck out the back. The gardens were more exposed after my work in them, and I didn't want to be seen walking through town in Beatrice's costume, so I would change closer to the party.

"Which way?" I whispered to Beatrice.

She guided me, glowing in the gibbous moon like a faint lantern in the darkness.

"You'll have to sneak in through the gardens again," she whispered. *"This house has a hedge maze. It's quite charming."*

She ushered me into the gardens, and I found a convenient hiding place to pull the gown over my shirt and trousers and put on a brown wig. I had no bronze angel with her basin, but Beatrice assured me that I looked well enough. I had worn the red slippers over to the house, not wanting to deal with boots. So all that was left was to don the mask.

"Perfect!" Beatrice breathed. *"I cannot wait to see how everyone reacts."*

My throat had gone dry, but music and laughter flowed from the house. For a moment, I could pretend to be a carefree guest.

"Yes, let's put this to the test."

CHAPTER 13

Beatrice guided me around the hedge maze. A few masked couples had chosen the gardens for their rendezvous, and they looked up from their sweet nothings to watch me pass. I didn't know if that was because of my costume or because they didn't want to be caught in their dalliances.

I entered the house through the garden doors, which led directly into the ballroom. The heat of the crush of bodies hit me like a wall. I stopped, pinned by the mob of dancers like a butterfly on a board. The smell of blood filled my nose, and I heard again the shouts for the guillotine to cut another life short.

"Charlotte!"

I inhaled sharply and brought myself back to the present. How could I think that I might enjoy myself at this ball? It was wrong, when people I loved suffered. I was only here to help Beatrice and Henri.

I hadn't intended my entrance to create a dramatic effect, but many heads turned to stare at my bright costume as I paused at the entrance.

I kept my chin up and walked through the press of their stares, making my way toward the drinks for lack of a better destination. But a ghost should not be thirsty. Instead, I swished around and stood at the side of the room to watch the dancers, allowing people to gawk at me and whisper.

No one shouted anything about ghosts or murder, nor did they rush to either confess their misdeeds or to kill me. No one spoke to me, either. I stood for some time like a strange adornment to the gathering. Sweat trickled down my back under the layers of clothing and costume, but I did my best to stand still and unconcerned and start rumors.

Beatrice left me to circulate through the dancers. She skirted the couples, but sometimes people stepped through her. One woman shivered and looked ill after a brush with Beatrice.

One pair of strolling ladies slowed down to stare. I caught snatches of their conversation.

"Doesn't that look like..."

"Bad taste."

I hoped my flush didn't show beneath the red of the mask. I hoped that Beatrice was gathering useful gossip.

"Pardon, my lady," said a deep baritone voice.

Lord Treverton.

I slowly rotated to face him. I could not be recognized, but he might remember my accent. I said nothing.

"May I have this dance?"

Denying him would require speaking or a very un-dignified retreat. If he was the killer, he might be trying to find out what I knew. I had come to distrust large gatherings, but he was unlikely to murder me in a crowded ballroom.

I inclined my head and took his hand. As I did, I caught a glimpse of Mrs. Medford looking very put out. Frances went into a semi-swoon, supported by Loretta.

Lord Treverton pulled me out to the floor. The dance was an allemande, so he held me close and studied my face. I was grateful for the protection of the mask.

"Have I met you before, my lady?"

I shrugged one shoulder.

"Being coy, are we?" he asked. He pulled me closer. Too close. I could feel the warmth of his body, and his gaze bored into me.

"Alas, poor ghost!" he whispered into my ear, his breath warm against my skin. A shiver raced through me.

I pushed back from him, glaring.

"No, I didn't think you were dead and past feeling." He smirked, his eyes searching mine. "Nevertheless, 'Speak. I am bound to hear.'"

He was quoting Hamlet. My line would be to tell him he was bound to revenge when he heard my tale. Did that mean that he had killed Beatrice? No, Hamlet was not the murderer, but the avenger. Did Treverton know or suspect something about Beatrice's death?

I lowered my voice, making it hoarse. "Do you know my tale?"

He narrowed his eyes. "The spirit does speak of revenge, then."

"Of truth," I murmured.

"And yet you come in deceit. You are no ghost. A ghost's skin would not warm when I touched it. And there is something more familiar about you than an old costume." He reached for my face. For my mask.

I spun away, breaking his grip on me, and dashed for the garden. He huffed and followed. If Beatrice could stop him, this was her time, but I would not count on that. I fled for the maze. One of my slippers came lose, but I kicked it behind me and kept running, my stockinged foot pounding over the rough gravel.

Once in the maze, I wound my way through, tossing aside the costume as I went. When I was finally back in my male disguise, and at a dead end, I found a weak spot in the hedge and wiggled my way through it to double back.

Lord Treverton's boots crunched on the gravel in the maze, and he panted when he stopped at the dead end. I put the one remaining slipper back on to cushion my foot and slipped as quietly as I could away from the maze.

A chuckle came from the other side of the hedge. I froze, afraid he had spotted me and I looked the fool.

He raised his voice. "I see by the trail you've left behind that when I find you, you will look quite different. Am I supposed to think you've vanished? I assume this empty gown isn't left to tease me."

I flushed in the darkness. It would certainly be extraordinary if I were running about the hedge maze in only my shift.

"Lost your voice again, spirit?" he called. "You cannot have gone far. I have your other slipper. And I am quite curious how you came upon this extraordinary costume. One does not forget it as quickly as you discarded it. If you want it back, you will have to trade it for information."

I waited in the silence that followed his declaration. The costume might have been useful to me again, but I would not reveal myself. He could keep the gown. I had to stifle a chuckle at an image of him wearing the elaborate, feathered mask.

"We have not seen the last of each other, Lady Spirit," he called.

The sound of his footsteps on gravel receded, but I stayed very still, not shifting even when my legs began to ache. I was afraid he was correct. We were not done with one another.

CHAPTER 14

I took slow, silent breaths as I waited to be sure Treverton was gone. Finally, I saw a faint light near the back wall of the garden. I crept over.

"It's safe," Beatrice whispered. *"Through here."*

I looked over my shoulder the entire walk back. Even Beatrice stayed quiet until we reached the Medfords' garden.

"What an astounding success!" Beatrice cried, clapping her insubstantial hands.

I laughed, releasing the tension in my shoulders. "You thought that was a success?"

"Yes. I still believe Lord Treverton could be the killer, don't you?"

"He could be," I conceded. "But I'm not sure. Something about the way he spoke made him sound more curious than guilty."

"Well, I saw others acting guilty. Mr. Hawke went deathly

white at the sight of you. And Lord Martin's eyes bulged, and he hurried out of the room."

"That does sound like guilty behavior from both of them. I've observed Hawke, but what do you remember of Lord Martin?"

"We often danced, and he sent me flowers and called on me. But he flirted with many girls, so I was never certain if he was serious. I didn't want him to be. His drinking and wild moods made me uneasy. I danced with him at the masquerade that last night, though."

"Tell me everything you remember from that ball."

Her eyes grew distant. *"It becomes hazy. I think the longer I'm trapped here, the less there is of me. But I danced almost every dance at the ball. It was a smashing success. I was very hopeful that Mr. Hawke was going to make me an offer."*

I thought of the couples lurking in the darkness of the garden. "Did you make it home that night?"

"I... I think I did. I was so happy, it was like I was floating. I changed out of my gown. I had my mother's brooch, and I needed to return it to her. That's..." Her eyes widened. *"That's something new I remember! I left the room with the brooch..."*

"Try to picture your path," I urged.

She squinted, her forehead wrinkled in concentration. *"I... it's dark."*

"Come!" I beckoned her toward the house. "The girls won't be home for hours. When my father forgot things, I had him retrace his whole route. Let's try it."

Beatrice nodded her approval, and we rushed back inside. The butler snoozed by the front door, but we snuck up the stairs.

"Which room was yours?" I whispered to Beatrice.

"The one Miss Loretta has now. My sister had the one next to it, and my brother had Miss Frances's room."

I tiptoed down the corridor to Loretta's room, Beatrice floating behind me. The door was unlocked, and we stepped into the dim chamber.

"Walk through that night again," I said.

Beatrice nodded. She mimed changing clothes and sending her maid away. Then she pretended to clutch the brooch.

"I called the maid, but she had already gone downstairs." She smiled. *"I hadn't remembered that before."*

"Good, keep going."

She stepped out into the corridor, pretending to hold the brooch. *"I walked toward my mother's room. But..."* She scrunched her forehead. *"I heard a noise out in the garden."* She stared hard at the window, then shook her head. *"No. That's all I can remember."*

I frowned. "Do you know, after you died, if your family had the brooch?"

"I don't... Actually, I think it was missing."

I scowled at the window. "Let's go back to the garden."

Beatrice shrugged and followed me outside.

"What kind of noise was it that you heard that night?" I asked her.

Her forehead scrunched. *"Voices, I think. Or a voice."*

"Talking to each other or calling you?"

She bit her lips in concentration, then turned large, sorrowful eyes to me. *"I just don't remember."*

"That's all right." I stared up at the window, trying to

gauge how close or how loud voices would have to be for her to hear them. "Do you think you would have gone outside?"

Her eyes brightened. *"Maybe. Not if I thought it was dangerous, but if I knew the voices."*

"Like if one of your suitors was calling you?" I asked with a smile.

"Yes, perhaps! Isn't that scandalous of me?" Her face fell. *"Of course, not as scandalous as being murdered."*

"True." She might have come to the garden for a rendezvous, but she also might have heard something dangerous. There were smugglers about, after all. "It gives us some ideas, at least."

I still felt like we had more questions than answers, and too many people to suspect.

CHAPTER 15

I roused slowly the next day, exhausted from running about in the dark. Voices drifted into my room from below. I recognized the deep baritone of Lord Treverton. The sound filled me with a thrill mingling excitement and dread. I sat up. Why on earth was he in this part of the house, so close to the bedchambers and the attic?

I crept over and knelt by the crack beneath the door to hear more.

"There was a tragedy here, you know," he said.

I froze. Was he going to confess?

"Really?" Frances tittered. "How exciting."

"Hmm." Treverton said. "A young woman went missing from this house. She was never found."

"Oh! Was that the girl they were talking about last night?" Frances asked. "They said she's a ghost."

"Do you believe in ghosts Miss Medford?"

"Of course! It would be dull not to."

"Indeed. Do you think this house is haunted?"

"Oh, yes, I'm sure I've heard any number of strange noises from the attic."

"Is the attic empty?"

"Of course! Only our cousin is staying there."

"I see," Treverton said, and I could feel his eyes turning to the attic, as if he could see directly through the door —and me.

How much did he know? He obviously guessed at least some of it or he wouldn't be prying. Was it because he was guilty and wanted to cover his trail? To silence me?

"Thank you for the tour, Mrs. Medford, Miss Medford," Lord Treverton said. "I wonder, before I go, if I might have a word with your cousin? A friend might be in need of tutoring for his progeny when you leave Lymouth."

"As long as you promise not to poach him from me before we leave," Mrs. Medford said. "He's working wonders with my girls."

"I can't promise anything. I hope you are treating the lad well?"

"Oh, yes. It's a privilege to offer shelter to an émigré. I have always been known for my generosity."

"Yes, offering a displaced aristocrat shelter in your attic. Very kind."

The sarcasm dripped from his voice, but Mrs. Medford murmured her agreement.

"Charles?" she called. "Lord Treverton would like a word with you."

I groaned and looked around. No sign of Beatrice. Maybe she was spying on Treverton. Not that she could protect me, but I would feel better if I knew someone was watching out for me. I arranged myself to look as masculine as possible, then clambered down the stairs.

Mrs. Medford wore a simpering smile, and Frances stood near Treverton with a possessive air.

Lord Treverton gestured to me. "Monsieur Cartier, isn't it? Come, walk with me."

I didn't want to, but how could I avoid it? I bowed to the ladies and followed Treverton onto the street.

He guided me to a spot overlooking the sea and the ruins of the ancient monastery where the rush of the waves would muffle our conversation. The stunning scene made my fingers itch for a pencil, but that was not why I was there.

"Well," Treverton said. "You have managed to capture my attention, but I hardly know what to call you."

"Cartier will work fine, my lord," I said.

He laughed. "You are maintaining that masquerade, then?"

I gave him my best stupid look.

He smirked and bent closer. "What if I kissed you in front of everyone, lovely spirit? That would ruin your little game."

My cheeks flamed. "Or ruin your reputation! What kind of lord kisses French tutors?" He clearly thought me a low sort of person if he threatened to kiss me in public.

"Ha! Anyone who believes you are only a tutor—and a male one at that—must be daft, but my eyes are open now."

He pulled the red slipper from a pocket in his coat, and I knew my case was hopeless.

He grinned. "I admit you fooled me at first. I thought you two people, a brother and sister perhaps, playing some sort of ruse on the Medfords. But switching back and forth between boy and lady made it too obvious, even with your wigs and masks. Your eyes are...difficult to forget. And your face is too delicate even for a boy. Now, I can't imagine how everyone doesn't see it."

I sighed. "They see what they expect."

"Hmm. That is true enough. What is your name, truly?"

"Charlotte Carter," I mumbled.

"Are you even a cousin of the Medfords?"

"Of course! They paid so little attention to my branch of the family..."

"That they didn't remember that their cousin was a girl and not a boy." His eyes brightened. "Oh, and I gave you the hint, didn't I? You *are* the French lad I met that night, and I warned you Mrs. Medford wouldn't like distractions. Competition. Is that why you did this?"

I shoved my hands in my pockets. "One of the reasons."

He swept me with a speculative glance. "Very well. If you will not satisfy my curiosity, I must decide what it will cost you to keep this secret."

I stared out across the Channel. Henri was out there somewhere, while Lord Treverton was playing games with me. "I have nothing to give you."

"That is a shame," he said with a wicked smile.

Would he reveal me? Yes. I believed he would, if only to amuse himself. "I can only say that I must stay hidden, my lord. A life is on the line."

"Really? How gothic." He studied me. "But you have gone quite pale. I believe you are telling the truth. Does this have to do with disguising yourself as a girl who vanished a year ago?"

"I am trying to discover what happened to her."

He lifted his quizzing glass and spun it on its chain. "You intrigue me, Carter. I will keep your secret for now, and in exchange, you will let me help you with your mystery."

I gave a start and stared at him. "You're going to help me? Why?"

"Not out of altruism, I assure you. I am bored. Society is dull. All of this is dull. But you are not dull, and neither is your little mystery."

I felt my hackles rise. "What a precious luxury, to be bored! To have no terrors weighing on your mind."

He regarded me thoughtfully. "What a precious luxury, to have some reason to care. Something to give your life meaning. So, you see, we will help each other."

I didn't want Lord Treverton's help. I didn't want anything to do with him. But I didn't think I had a choice. "How do you expect to help me?"

"First, you have to tell me what brought you here and why you care about the missing girl. You really are a refugee from France. Your drawing convinced me of that."

"I am." He would laugh at me if I admitted I talked to ghosts, or else think I was lying and become offended. Then he might reveal my secret. "I am trying to make my way here. But I stumbled across Beatrice...Miss Foley's mystery, and it...haunts me."

"Beatrice, is it? You're intimately acquainted? Did she flee to France to start a new life with a lover, then?"

"No. I firmly believe she is dead." I glanced over my

shoulder. "I think she stumbled across information she shouldn't have and someone killed her for her efforts."

"You have made a great deal of headway in your investigation."

"I am living in the same house as the missing girl," I said. "Tell me what you know, if we're going to work together."

"Miss Beatrice Foley was the toast of the town last year. She had several love sick men dangling after her. In addition to a pleasing face and temperament, she had a respectable fortune. Then, at the height of her popularity, she disappeared. It was all anyone talked about for weeks. I believe most had forgotten until you appeared again in her gown last night. How did you know to do that?"

"She...left a diary." I hurried over the lie. "The last entry was after the ball. She had a jewel to return to her mother and...that was it."

"I always suspected she absconded with a footman or something equally mundane. The missing jewel—a brooch, I believe—was part of the story. They said she took it to fund her new life. It is still missing." He frowned. "But if her journal was truthful, something dark befell her."

"Did you care for her?" I asked, surprised to find I was a little jealous. I had no time to worry over a rake's interests. Yet beneath his blasé demeanor, there lurked intelligence and a spark of curiosity that resonated with me.

He laughed. "Oh, for an evening, as a pretty girl to flirt with. I was not one of her earnest suitors."

"But you care what happened to her."

"As I said, I am bored. I'm certain with a little work, we can uncover the truth, and that will be amusing for another evening." He glanced at me. "Are you going to tell me I'm heartless?"

I shrugged one shoulder. "You already know it, and I admit you have resources I do not."

"Yes. For instance, access to her former suitors and even her brother."

"You know her family?"

"I know her brother a little. The rest of the family chose to stay away from Lymouth this year, but her brother has returned."

"Do you think he knows anything?"

"The whole family searched for her. They were torn apart by her loss, not the least because it cast a shadow on their reputation."

"Hmph." Did no one actually care that Beatrice was murdered, or was it only entertaining or inconvenient for them?

"Your appearance at the ball has everyone talking again. I think we might be able to discover new gossip if, as you say, someone actually harmed the girl."

"How will we do that?" I asked.

"Let me think on it. I'll reach you at the Medfords' house."

With that, I was dismissed, though at least I had news to share with Beatrice.

CHAPTER 16

I returned to the house to find Mrs. Medford watching from the drawing room window. She frowned at the sight of me, and I hunched my shoulders under her disapproving gaze. No point in trying to sneak around the back way; they knew I had gone out, and they knew I had returned.

The butler escorted me to the drawing room.

Mrs. Medford pounced on me like a cat after a mouse, catching my arm in a tight grip. "You walked with Lord Treverton. What did he want to speak about?"

I glanced behind her, where Frances lay on the sofa, pouting and fanning herself.

"He wanted to know more of my background." That was true enough.

"He asked about my girls, though."

I tried to understand what she expected me to say, what

white lie would satisfy her. "Uh, he inquired after their health. Which I told him was excellent."

She stared me down. "Did he ask about the missing girl, Miss Foley?"

He had been speaking about her with Mrs. Medford present, so it seemed a dangerous thing to lie about.

"He asked if I had known her."

Mrs. Medford hmphed and released my arm. "He showed an interest in her last year. I do not want him distracted. You are not to speak with him about her, do you understand?"

I nodded, because it was more comfortable to lie through actions than words.

Mrs. Medford sat on the sofa and stroked her daughter's arm. "I have it on good authority that Lord Treverton's grandfather, the earl, has required him to end his wild ways and marry. He encourages Treverton to look to our family because of his great friendship with the girls' grandfather. If Lord Treverton does want to speak with you, you must extoll the virtues of your cousins—especially Frances."

I bowed my head. I did not wish to harm Frances's future opportunities, but I couldn't bring myself to promise to extol her virtues. "I'm sure he does not regard my opinion, madam."

"No, and why should he?" She waved her hand. "If you're not going to be useful, go back to the attic."

I nodded and hurried upstairs, seething at the Medfords, Treverton, and myself. Treverton had no reason to discuss his matrimonial plans with me, and I had no desire to play matchmaker. I probably ought to be pleased to think of Treverton shackled to my cousin. They deserved each other.

No, that was unfair. Frances—and Loretta—had suffered with the loss of their father. I ought to do all that I could to help them. But would marrying Treverton really be a favor to anyone? Better to live in poverty than with such an arrogant man!

Beatrice appeared behind me, her eyes bright with interest.

"What did Lord Treverton really say?" she asked as soon as I had closed the attic door.

I sighed and sat on my bed. "He knows about my ruse. But he wants to help solve your mystery. He said we could speak to your brother."

"My brother is here?" Beatrice asked. *"Oh, I would love to see him again. Do you think he'll be able to see me?"*

"I don't know." It would be interesting if he could. Maybe I'd have some real assistance in solving her murder. "Tell me about your brother."

"There's a picture of him in my sketchbook—the one you've been using!"

"Oh, this was yours?" I opened the sketchbook and flipped through it. "You have some skill. You just have to learn to stick to one subject."

"Yes, I should have."

I winced. Beatrice would not be improving her sketching skills anymore. At least, not with the tools available in this world.

I flipped through the drawings. Treverton. Hawke. Maybe Lord Martin?

"There!" Beatrice pointed to a drawing of a handsome but distant man. *"That's William. He's quite a few years older than*

me. Strange as it may seem, I didn't know him well. He was always off at school, and then it seemed as if he didn't have time for a little sister. I wish I had known him better. But perhaps this is my chance. Maybe that's why I'm still here, to heal the family bonds."

William Foley didn't sound like he would have much reason to see Beatrice now, if he'd hardly noticed her when he was alive, but I didn't want to dash her hopes.

"When are you going to speak with Lord Treverton again?"

I groaned to myself. "Soon, no doubt."

"Could he be the murderer and trying to throw you off track? Or murder you as well?"

"If he wanted to murder me, he could have done it today. Or simply revealed me and discredited me with everyone." Murder might have been more humane, except I needed to save Henri. "He is bored, and this amuses him."

"Well, that seems quite heartless of him, but I hope he's able to help anyway."

As did I.

We only had a day to wait before Treverton returned to visit the Miss Medfords. This time, I sought no excuse to leave the drawing room so he could speak to me if he had information. Frances flirted with Treverton until it set my teeth on edge. Why did I care? I ignored them and focused on my drawing of Loretta. Despite her smile, I couldn't make her eyes look anything but sad.

"Charlotte!" Beatrice warned.

Treverton wandered in my direction. "Your drawing skills are excellent."

I looked up at him, expecting to find mockery in his gaze. He looked amused, but not mocking.

"Thank you, sir," I said.

"I know someone who would like to commission an artist. Come, let me tell you the details."

Frances watched with a pout as Treverton led me away from the party. Why would she be jealous? As far as she knew, I was a boy, and Treverton was most definitely interested in women. Could she just not bear to share a moment of his attention?

Yet as I walked by his side into the corridor, he stayed close to me, a sort of friendly intimacy that made my stomach do strange things. It was only that we shared a secret. That would always create a bond—but one that would be easily broken when Treverton grew bored again.

"Do you really know of a commission?" I asked him when we were alone—alone except for Beatrice. The money would be helpful.

He chuckled. "No, you'll have to find your own work if you want it—though I suspect you could, with your skills. Do you play cards?"

"Um." I did not play well, but Beatrice waved frantically at me.

"I play, and I can help you win."

"I play a little," I said.

"Excellent. Then you will join me tomorrow night at a friendly card game with some regular visitors to Lymouth. It will give you a chance to find gossip that you cannot hear at balls when ladies are present."

"What makes you think they will talk about Miss Foley?"

"Because I will invite her brother. I will tell him to arrive a little later than the other men, which will allow time for the gentlemen to gossip about him."

"*My brother!*"

"Will they, though?"

He laughed. "Ladies have the reputation for gossip, but men like it just as well. You must be prepared for some shocking language. Men speak much differently when ladies are not present."

"I am not a lady. Not an English one, at least. I will not be shocked." I couldn't allow myself to be. "But what if one of them sees me as a female?"

"Then *I* will pretend to be quite shocked, and the game is up."

I didn't like it, but I did need to get closer to the men we suspected. And if Beatrice helped me win, I could earn some money to help Henri. "Very well."

Treverton bowed, his gaze lingering on me longer than necessary, then returned to the ladies. The other ladies.

Mrs. Medford caught me with a whisper. "Don't let any other work take you away from your duties tutoring my girls."

"No, of course not, madam. But some art commissions might allow me to be less reliant on your hospitality. I know you cannot wish me to remain your guest forever."

"Certainly not," she said.

And she left me alone.

I turned to where Beatrice hovered with a smile.

She clapped her hands. "*I will finally see some of my family again! I wonder if my brother misses me much. If he is in Lymouth seeking answers."*

"It seems Lord Treverton sees your brother only as bait for the conversation," I whispered, "though I hope it does you good to see him again. This should be a good opportunity to find out more about our suspects. But you will have to teach me to play cards now."

CHAPTER 17

After a few card lessons with Beatrice and practicing with the Miss Medfords—always letting them win—I was as prepared as possible for Treverton's card party. The moon waned in the night sky, reminding me that Henri's month was almost up.

Mrs. Medford caught me on my way out the garden door. "Where are you going? If you're in need of something to occupy yourself, the rugs in the corridors need to be taken out and cleaned."

"Lord Treverton invited me out," I said quickly. "I thought it would be an opportunity to help." I didn't mention who I would be helping.

Her eyes narrowed. "Very well."

I bowed and hurried away, arriving at Lord Treverton's lodgings at exactly the time the invitation stated.

"No one else will be so prompt," Beatrice warned as I knocked on the door.

Treverton's valet answered and showed me in. The man disappeared somewhere in the back of the apartments, and Treverton came forward, giving me a speculative look.

"No one else is here yet, you know," he said.

"*I told you.*"

"I wanted a little time to settle my mind before the others arrive," I said.

"Settle away. You brought coin, I assume? They may not be quick to accept you as a gentleman, which means they'll hesitate to take your vowels."

"*Your IOU,*" Beatrice reminded me.

"I brought coin," I said.

I hoped that with Beatrice's help, I would come away with more. I couldn't win all the time, but she could nudge me to lose less and win more.

"Excellent. Will you have some wine? Or brandy?"

"I would rather keep my head clear."

Because it suddenly occurred to me that I was alone with a gentleman of questionable reputation in his chambers, and I had only his word that he had invited others. By the curious way he watched me, I wondered if the same thing had occurred to him.

He swirled the wine in his glass. "You never told me why you were so interested in this girl's death."

I glanced at Beatrice, who shrugged.

"*Tell him whatever you wish.*"

"It's wrong that she disappeared and no one ever found what happened to her," I said. "If no one else will help her, I will."

"I see. You are also bored and looking for something to occupy your mind." He took a long sip of wine.

"Not all of us have the luxury of being bored, *sir*," I snapped.

"Ha! Think you'll put me in my place, do you?"

"That's not my concern. I have enough problems of my own without taking on yours."

"Come, what troubles could you have? You're in England now, safe, and with an interesting new identity."

"Interesting?" I gestured to my waistcoat and cravat. "You think I'm doing this out of choice? I would much rather be myself, but... but not everyone I care for is out of harm's way. I have to protect the people I love."

"Ah." His expression cooled. "You left a lover behind in France. Is he some mincing aristocrat relying on you to save him? Or one of the bloody revolutionaries who got in over his head?"

"Neither! It's my younger brother. He's..." I gritted my teeth. This was none of his affair, but I didn't like the aspersions he cast on my character. "He's in danger and relying on me."

He set his wine glass aside and frowned at it. "You have such loyalty. That must be delightful."

"You could choose to be loyal and find out."

"No doubt." He flashed a rueful half-smile. "But I meant it would be delightful to have someone I could trust to be loyal to me."

"Oh."

Did he not have a loyal friend? No, perhaps he did not. If he was a scoundrel sought for his money and title more than for himself, he might not be able to trust anyone's loyalty. At least I had that: Henri loved me. He counted on me. I had to remember that—remember why I was doing this.

Another knock sounded on the door, and the valet opened it to admit a group of three men: Hawke, Lord Martin, and another gentleman I recognized from the dance floor.

Beatrice moved back as if afraid they would see her.

"Treverton!" Hawke called. "You see, we have come for cards. I hope you have been drinking, because we have, and it won't be a fair game if you're not foxed as well."

Treverton held up his glass. "My friend Carter and I have just been indulging. Martin and Goring, may I present to you Charles Carter, a French gentleman lately escaped from the troubles across the Channel."

Hawke nodded a friendly greeting.

Lord Martin eyed me with something that amounted to drunk sympathy. "Rough go of it, eh, my fellow? What, are you some aristocrat escaped the bed of Madame Guillotine, then?"

"Something like that. Glad to be in England," I said, making my voice gruff. Though these men were probably not at their most observant. Treverton had purposely invited them at a time they would be drunk and therefore have looser tongues and weaker eyes.

"Come, have some wine," Treverton invited the other men.

Lord Martin grabbed a glass.

Hawke eyed him dubiously. "I don't know why you drink

so heavily when you play. I shouldn't complain, since it usually comes out to my advantage."

Martin shrugged, sloshing his wine. "I enjoy drinking, and I enjoy playing cards. Why not do as much of both as I please, eh, Treverton?"

I took a glass as well, careful not to drink more than a sip so I could keep my head clear. The men rambled on about hunting and gambling and country estates. Far from shocking; I found it quite dull.

"When do you bring out the cards?" Hawke asked.

"We're waiting on one more," Treverton said. "Mr. Foley."

The men nodded.

"One more glass, then, Treverton," Lord Martin slurred. "This is excellent wine. Must be French, eh? From the 'free traders?'"

"I request it, and my man delivers. I don't ask any questions."

Lord Martin brayed out a laugh. "We're in a smuggling town. Buy the best of everything here for less coin."

The men spoke of wine and brandy for a few minutes, then Treverton checked his watch.

"Foley is quite rude to keep us so long. I suppose we shouldn't start without him. Wouldn't want him to miss out on his fair chance to lose his money."

The men laughed at this.

"Wonder how he's been. It was a shame about his sister," Hawke said slowly. "At the time, I thought she was the prettiest thing I'd ever seen. I might have married her."

"Did you hear that?" Beatrice drifted closer to the men. *"He* was *going to marry me!"*

Before anyone could ask Hawke who was prettier now, Treverton said, "Did Miss Foley never turn up, then? I thought she had eloped."

"Everyone thought so for a while," Lord Martin slurred, "but time has gone by, and there's neither hide nor hair of her."

"I never thought it of her," Hawke mumbled into his wine.

"Did anyone else vanish at the same time? Some gentlemen or adventurer?" Treverton asked.

Lord Martin shook his head. "No, there was never a whisper of anything about her. It's like she walked off into the mist and the Fair Folk took her."

"More likely some brigand cut her throat," Treverton said.

The other men gasped in protest, and Beatrice scowled.

"I hate to think of such a pretty girl dead," Goring said.

"Never found a body," Lord Martin slurred.

"Maybe she found herself in trouble and her family whisked her away," Treverton suggested.

"That girl! No, she was jolly but innocent. And her brother kept a close eye on her," Goring said.

Beatrice nodded vigorously. *"Thank you!"*

Hawke said little. In fact, I thought he seemed rather guilty, hunkered down in his chair. Maybe he did know more than he was letting on. And he had missed the assembly ball on the same night the smugglers were sighted.

A knock sounded on the door, and the valet admitted Mr. Foley. Beatrice's sketch was faithful: he was as handsome as she was pretty, but his eyes were reserved where hers were bright.

"Oh, my brother! I have missed the sight of my family."

Foley paused for a moment, looking confused, but then he shook his head. Had he heard her, too? I could hardly ask, but I watched him closely.

"Foley, welcome!" Treverton said—jumping in before anyone could chastise him for being very late, I noticed. "We were just wondering if there was any word on your pretty young sister. I hope she has returned safe to her family."

Foley's face fell. "I wish you would not ask such things! It has been a terrible sorrow for all of us, and I can only think her dead. What else would keep her from her family for so long? It plagues me that I was not able to protect her."

The men hastened to assure him he could not have foreseen whatever calamity had befallen her, that he was an excellent brother, that perhaps she would turn up alive and well after all.

"He does care about me!" Beatrice said happily. *"He always seemed to think me such a nuisance."*

I watched him brush off the attention from the others. It was easier to express affection for someone when they were no longer around, but he did seem upset, and he waved off the questions.

"Please, this talk puts me at a disadvantage. I don't wish to mourn while I play cards."

With murmurs of agreement, the men and I settled in to play cards. With Beatrice's help, I came out ahead—enough for the men to declare me lucky, but not enough for them to declare me a cheater. Though, cheater I was, since Beatrice looked at the other men's cards and told me how to bet and what cards to take.

A few times, I thought her brother might have heard a whisper of her voice. He played a dull game and lost quite a few coins.

I couldn't count my coins there at the table, but I was at least a few pounds closer to freeing my brother. At the expense of my honesty, but I told myself this was just a game to these men—coins they would hardly miss—while I needed every shilling I could scrounge for Henri.

I considered the night a success, and was happy enough to take my winnings and prepare to leave when the other men stumbled out.

"You had quite a successful night," Treverton said, catching me before I could leave.

"God favors children and fools."

"He must, because I can tell by the way you hold your cards that you are not an experienced card player."

Beatrice motioned me toward the door, but I could hardly turn and flee from Treverton. He would catch me.

"Just lucky," I said.

"I don't believe in luck. You are keeping too many secrets from me."

"They are mine to keep. You have not earned any of them."

"There you are wrong. I helped you tonight, and I'm suspicious that you've played me a bad hand in return."

"You want some of the money?" I asked, disappointed to think I might lose what progress I had made toward freeing my brother. A few more games like these, and I might not have to steal anything.

"No, I want my curiosity scratched. Come, tell me how you did it."

"I practiced with the Miss Medfords."

He barked out a harsh laugh. "They could not have taught you to play so well. If you want more help from me, you will have to tell me your secret."

I looked at Beatrice, who shrugged helplessly.

"Very well. You want to know my secret? I can see Miss Foley's ghost. She is here is the room with me right now, and she told me when to bet and when to abstain."

Treverton's eyes narrowed. "I don't like your humor."

Beatrice looked panicked, and she sailed through the house, vanishing into a neighboring room.

"His valet is drinking from his best wine this very instant," Beatrice called.

"Your valet is stealing your wine!" I said.

Treverton blinked. "What?"

"Miss Foley told me to tell you that."

He frowned. "I have known him to do so, but you may have guessed that."

"There is a portrait of a pretty young lady in his bed chamber."

I raised my eyebrows. Of course there was. "Whose portrait do you keep near your bed? Miss Foley says she is lovely."

He glanced over his shoulder, then back at me, his brows drawn in confusion. "Does she? What excellent taste she has, then. Or were you peeking in my chambers?" His face darkened. "Planning to set out your lures for me like all the other title-hunting females?"

I flushed. "Not at all!"

"Very well." He said coolly and put his hand out of sight. "How many fingers am I holding behind my back?"

"None," Beatrice told me.

"You're not holding up any."

Treverton drew his hand back out and stared at me. Then he glanced about the room. "There is a ghost here, then?"

"There is."

He shook his head. "I have had too much to drink. Perhaps this is all just a strange dream. Go away. I will speak to you again when I feel up to it."

I did, happy to flee from Lord Treverton.

CHAPTER 18

The next morning, I went out to the garden early to sit at the bronze angel's feet and sketch her. I spent extra time capturing the details of her face. They blurred with my memories of my mother's features, and I could imagine she still watched over me.

Treverton had given me the idea of trying to sell my drawings. I was so close to having enough to free Henri. And if the local gentry hired me to draw portraits, it would also give me a chance to spy on more people in Lymouth. Yet I was tempted to keep this drawing. I'd been thinking over Beatrice's questions, and I found that I did enjoy sketching—not just because it made me useful. It gave me another way to understand the world. A way to escape into my thoughts and put them in order.

My stomach tightened, and I pushed the glimmer of happiness away. I was being selfish. I had to sell this drawing if I could. It was wrong to pursue my own pleasures when I had so many responsibilities.

Beatrice rushed over to me from the house.

"You'd best come inside. Lord Treverton is scheming something."

"Oh dear." I set my sketch aside and snuck in behind Beatrice. What trouble was he causing now?

Treverton's voice came from the drawing room. I lurked closer to hear.

"A party would be an excellent idea, Miss Medford. I wish I had thought of it." By his smug tone, I was certain he'd put the idea in her head.

"Oh, we can host a cozy party, can't we, Mother?" Frances said. I could almost hear her batting her eyelashes. "With cards and dancing?"

"Well, if Lord Treverton would enjoy it, then how can we say no?" Mrs. Medford's voice dripped with a simpering desire to please, though I doubted she could afford to host a party when I knew how they economized.

I rolled my eyes. Would Treverton always get his way?

"And we can be selective about whom we invite," Frances said.

"Ha, that would mean you're not welcome," Beatrice said.

I nodded, but it didn't matter if they wouldn't invite the mystery woman—I was already here and would be able to eavesdrop. Perhaps that was Treverton's intention. Or maybe he liked Frances's fawning ways and was only looking out for himself. It would please his grandfather the earl if he selected her as his bride.

"We should extend charity to our less fortunate neighbors," Mrs. Medford said.

"Oh, I don't mind about them," Frances said airily.

Yes, she definitely wanted to exclude me. I was tempted to show up as the mystery woman just to infuriate her, but who knew what she might do? And if she recognized me, both Henri and Beatrice had no one else to help them.

I left Beatrice to eavesdrop further and went back to the garden to think of the best way to turn this party to my advantage. If I put some drawings on display, I might get commissions.

Treverton strutted into the garden alone, looking supremely pleased with himself.

"You've been scheming," I said.

"How did you know?"

"Aside from your smugness? Miss Foley told me."

He looked around the garden. "Is she here now?"

"No. I don't always know where she goes."

"Hmm." He sat next to me on the bench, forcing me to scoot over so I didn't rub shoulders with him. "It was my older sister."

"What?"

"The portrait you asked about. The one by my bedside. Unless I was more drunk than I thought, and my memory addled."

My curiosity stirred. "No, Miss Foley did mention a portrait."

"Both of my parents are dead. My sister was like a mother to me."

"Oh?" I wasn't sure where he was going with this explanation.

"She married a man who was that rare combination of wealthy and kind. It seemed that everything in her life was secure." He gripped the edge of the bench and lowered his voice. "But then she died in childbirth."

"I'm sorry," I said, a little shocked at his sincere show of emotion.

"I learned there was no amount of goodness that can keep one safe. The promise of heaven seemed a cruel jest. I decided to find whatever amusement I could in the time I was granted in this world."

He stared blankly ahead, his thoughts somewhere far away. I wasn't certain how to react. I had done many things wrong in the last six months, not considering anything beyond surviving the day. It was hard to think of heaven when one's belly ached and the screams of hatred and madness haunted one's dreams. And what was I to do, when others relied on me, no matter the cost?

"I lost my mother as a child, and my father to the guillotine," I said.

"That must have been terrible." He shifted so his arm touched mine, and I didn't move away from the warmth. "Yet if Miss Foley's ghost is here, perhaps our loved ones are not entirely lost to us. It would mean that, wouldn't it?"

"I have thought the same. She says she can't see any other... spirits. But I have wondered if that's because she's trapped here. And if there's a *here*, there must also be a *there*. But..." I clenched my fists. "But if my father is out there somewhere, why hasn't he helped me?"

Treverton blinked at my outburst. "Perhaps he trusted that you could manage without help."

My eyes stung. "It never occurred to him before that I might need help. I always took care of Henri, and Father expected me to take care of him, too, while he was lost in his studies. Maybe he just drifted off on the other side and forgot all about me."

I buried my face in my hands and fought the tears. I would not cry. I always had to hold everything together—myself, Henri, everything. I loved my father, was proud of his brilliance, but the pain and betrayal were still real and raw, the burdens he left me with too heavy on my shoulders.

A soft touch brushed my back. I gave a start and looked at Treverton, who pulled his hand away like I was some startled animal that might bite.

"I'm here," he said carefully. "I'm helping you."

I wrapped my arms around myself. "As long as it amuses you."

He frowned and stared at the bronze angel, at the green patina streaking her face like tears. "I would truly be a cad if I deserted you now."

I shrugged. He *would* be a cad, but that's what everyone said of him already. It would not be the first time someone had forgotten me. Father often had, and what of the rest of my family—aside from Henri? My cousins didn't even know I was supposed to be a girl. I longed to believe I could rely on Treverton, but I had never known how to trust anyone but myself.

Treverton's expression brightened. "Miss Foley's ghost is a fascinating development. I am more interested than ever in solving her murder—for murder it must be. And she doesn't know what happened to her?"

I rubbed my eyes. "No. She doesn't remember. I've wondered if she never knew what happened."

"Why can you see her and no one else can?"

"I thought her brother heard her for a moment at the card game. But she thinks I can see her because I have also suffered—a sympathetic soul, so to speak."

"And you've been sharing her space, her wardrobe. That costume!"

"Her idea. I promised I would help her move on. It's not fair for anyone to be trapped like that."

"That's quite an obligation to take upon yourself."

"I'm certain all obligations seem like a burden to you," I snapped.

"Not so! Hence my reason for encouraging the Medfords to hold a party. The guilty person may wish to return here, to gloat over his work. Being in the same location could draw out some further sign of guilt."

I hadn't considered that. "So, the murderer may return and reveal something. And we'll be watching for him."

After a thoughtful pause, Treverton's lips curled up at one corner. "By we, I hope you mean yourself and the ghost."

A warmth I hadn't been aware of died like a snuffed candle, and my shoulders sagged. "I thought you were attending."

"Yes." He leaned closer, his scent of orange water encircling me. "Which means I will be dancing, of course. I can't let my host and her lovely daughters down. Or my grandfather the earl. He holds my purse strings, and he expects me to end my dissolute ways and marry. Choose my future countess. As I'm sure you've heard?"

"Of course," I grumbled.

"You can't wish me to be irresponsible."

"It's not my concern."

"Not even a little?" he asked, his voice low.

He met my gaze, searching my face for something. For a moment, the intensity of his green eyes drew me in, like we shared some secret that no one else could fathom.

But he was one of Society's darlings, a spoiled flirt. And I was no one.

I rolled my eyes and picked up my sketchbook, trying to end the conversation. Yet he lingered, watching me sketch until I grunted and turned to hide my drawing from him.

He laughed and stood. "Very well, I'm dismissed. Until later, my lady."

My face warmed at his familiar tone. Did he not think how dangerous it was to flirt with me, especially in my boy guise? As if I were just another—what did he call it?—title-hunting female. I had briefly considered swallowing my pride long enough to beg him for the money to help Henri, but then he would think me a fortune seeker and snub me and Beatrice—or perhaps betray me.

He bowed and sauntered away, a smile sparkling in his eyes. Insufferable man.

I ought to have been thankful that Treverton had orchestrated the party, but all I could imagine was him dancing with lovely girls while I skulked in the corridors. If I showed up as the mystery woman, would Treverton want to dance with me, too? I mentally shook myself. I was doing this for Beatrice and for Henri. What did it matter what I wanted?

CHAPTER 19

"We must not delay preparing for our little party!" Mrs. Medford announced that afternoon as I sat with my cousins working on their French. "Girls, we will freshen up your dresses with new ribbon. Lord Treverton will be sure to dance with you both since he encouraged this idea. He would be a good match for either of you."

"Loretta will probably steal him away from me," Frances said. "She's so much prettier than I am, and younger. He's sure to favor her."

Loretta gaped at her sister and fumbled over a protest.

"Now, dear, don't fret yourself," Mrs. Medford said, patting Frances's hand. "You are just as lovely as your sister, and as the oldest, of course it's right that Lord Treverton should pay you the most attention. If you decide you don't like him well enough, you may pass him on to Loretta, but we will have him as a match for one of you. His grandfather urges it."

Frances's eyes lit. "Countess. That does sound delightful."

"Heaven help us!" Beatrice exclaimed.

Frances's gaze fell on me and the sketchbook I always kept by my side. "Cousin Charles is so good at sketching. He could make drawings to show us to our best advantage. Hang them about the house to remind everyone who this party is for."

"It would be my pleasure." I had already hoped to draw attention to my sketches, and it would not hurt to have Frances showing them off. Her neighbors might commission me to make their spoiled daughters look sweet as well.

If there was a card room during the party, I could appear as Charles and win a little more money. I had counted and recounted my coins, praying I would have a few more pounds by the time the smugglers returned in a week. If I failed at selling my drawings or winning at cards, I would have to resort to more desperate measures.

"And your cousin Charles will help you practice your dancing," Mrs. Medford added.

I ran through the dances in my mind, but when the male and female parts differed, I became lost. Oh, dear. That would be sure to give me away. "I'm afraid I don't know English dances well, madam."

Her eyes narrowed. "Well, we can't have you be useless to your cousins. If you're not able to help in ballroom, you can help in the kitchen."

I stared at her. The cook had already made it clear she did not want me in her domain, and boys were not usually sent to the kitchens.

"The extra wine I ordered has arrived," she said slowly, as if I were stupid. "Go help bring it in."

"Yes, madam," I said through clenched teeth.

I took my sketchbook with me, thinking I might draw in peace when they weren't looking.

"*It is brutish the way she treats you,*" Beatrice fumed as she followed me to the kitchen.

I had trouble forming a defense of my cousins, so I shrugged her comment off. Instead, I put a half-formed idea into words.

"I think I might also draw some sketches of Lymouth for the party. And add you in the background."

"*Oh, me? I would love to be in one of your sketches. Thank you!*"

I smiled at her enthusiasm. "Well, you ought not be forgotten, and it might get people talking." I couldn't count on Treverton to help Beatrice at the party, since he would be busy enjoying himself.

"*Your cousins will hate it.*"

"I know." I felt utterly wicked for it, but it made me grin. I just had to be careful not to make it obvious or upset Mrs. Medford.

The cook looked up at me suspiciously when I entered her realm.

"I'm supposed to help bring in the wine," I told her.

The cook grunted. "It's out back."

I found a young lad already carrying crates of wine bottles into the kitchen.

"It's an awful big order of wine," he said. "Must not have all come here through the customs men, you know."

Smuggled wine. It was common enough from what I understood, and my aunt wasn't likely to wind up in trouble over it. The gentry rarely had legal troubles, except for debt. Henri, on the other hand, could be hanged just for being forced into the smuggler's proximity. For a moment, I understood the anger that stirred the mobs in France. But I would never condone their violence.

"I suppose you deliver much more wine than can be accounted for by the legal trade," I said to the lad.

He grinned. "I keep my back turned so I don't see anything."

"Of course." That was the rule to stay safe. Don't see anything.

He nodded toward my sketchbook, which I had left open on the table. "That's good. It's better than the ones I see in the bookseller's window."

I perked up. "Does he sell drawings?"

"I suppose. I got no reason to go inside, since I don't read. But he makes prints of nice pictures, and I like looking at them."

"That's good to know. Thank you," I said, wondering about this bookseller. Maybe he could help me sell my drawings.

"I'm good at noticing things," the boy told me, then an edge entered his voice. "Not like the sorts that throw these big parties."

I nodded. The gentry wouldn't notice something if it wasn't convenient. But what if Beatrice had seen something the night she died? She was bright and curious. I still thought that was the most likely explanation for her death.

The gentry wouldn't see Henri, either, except as a smuggler's associate. That was why he needed me. Treverton said he wanted to help, but Henri's predicament probably wasn't amusing enough for him.

So, when I had helped bring all the wine inside, I gave the boy the sketch he had admired, and then I collected my best ones from the house. I hesitated over the angel, tracing my careful lines, then steeled myself and added it with the others.

I made sure the Medfords were distracted, then snuck out to Lymouth's High Street, where the bookseller had his shop.

I entered the shop and paused to let my eyes adjust to the dimmer light. The scent of paper greeted me, and I let it roll over me before I took in the shop.

The proprietor stood behind his counter, wiping it with quick, nervous flicks of his rag. The only other customer was a thin, sour-faced gentleman with sharp eyes.

I straightened my spine and did my best boy swagger to the counter.

The proprietor glanced up warily, something like a warning in his eyes. I hesitated, but I needed to get more money for Henri, and I didn't know when I would be able to come again.

"Good morning, sir," I said. "I'm an artist, and I wondered if I might sell my sketches in your shop."

The bookseller looked annoyed, but he held out a hand for the sketches. The picture of the bronze angel rested on top.

His face softened as he studied the angel and then sorted

through the others. "These are quite good. I can sell them on commission for you."

"Thank you, sir!"

The bookseller set to work writing up a contract, and I felt the sharp-eyed man watching me. He stepped closer, and my back itched at his scrutiny.

"You are French," the man said, an accusation in his tone.

"Yes, sir," I said carefully, trying to keep my accent minimal.

"Do you still have contacts in your home country?"

Ah, I sensed a trap. Did he think I was a spy? "My mother was French, but my father was English. France is behind me, and I am home now."

"Do you know of other émigrés in Lymouth? A young woman, perhaps?"

They were looking for the mystery woman. I picked up a book from the counter so my fingers would not tremble. "I do not mingle much with company here. The only ladies I've met have been English."

"And do you know anything about smugglers here in England?"

What had Treverton and the delivery boy warned me? Don't look, then you don't have to lie. "I heard about the smugglers they almost caught, but I didn't see them."

The man watched me narrowly, no doubt aware of the tricks the smugglers and the townspeople used.

I signed the bookseller's contract and hurried out of the store, a cold sweat prickling the back of my neck. That man couldn't know about my brother, and I didn't want any more attention. I had too many secrets to keep hidden.

CHAPTER 20

The Medfords held their party a couple of days later. I made certain my sketches were displayed to good effect. The portraits of Frances and Loretta took the place of honor in the entrance hall, but I hung my other drawings throughout the main floor. I had worked Beatrice into the background of several—not making her obvious, but clear enough that someone who knew her would notice the likeness. Then I lingered with Beatrice in the background, feeling as invisible as her as we watched how guests reacted to seeing the house.

The ladies arrived in their delicate muslin gowns and the gentlemen in knee breeches and coat tails, some with powdered hair and some without. It was not a large gathering, and most gave no indication that they remembered the girl who had gone missing from the house the previous year. One couple whispered about it, but only as curious gossip, a passing thought as they moved on to affairs of the present.

Treverton approached and leaned against the wall next to me. Beatrice let out a huff and floated off to haunt the guests. The glow from the candles caught the gold in Treverton's hair as he smiled down at me. A strange lightness ran through me, but I forced it quiet.

"You're not dressed for a party," he said.

I shot him a withering glare. "I'm not invited."

"That never stopped you before, and I had hoped I might dance with you."

"You would look very foolish dancing with the household tutor."

He grinned. "You think that would stop me? But it wasn't a tutor I wanted to dance with. It was you."

My face warmed. What nonsense. "I am a tutor. A servant. That's all."

He looked at me more closely, keeping his voice low. "You can't possibly believe that. Not a clever woman who escapes revolutions and comes to the aid of ghosts."

I shook my head. I had never been anything but helpful. Useful. Quietly doing what must be done. Treverton made me sound almost heroic, but if I was what he said, it was simply because I had to be.

"Don't you wish to dance?" he asked, searching my face.

"I am only here to do what I must," I whispered.

"Hmm."

He looked disappointed, and my heart twinged to see it. Maybe it was only because I had hoped I might be what he thought me. Maybe I was a little disappointed with myself.

Before I could think of some way to amend my mistake, he tilted his head toward the sketch of Frances. "It's not much like her. Too innocent an expression. Oh, don't get angry with me—it's a good strategy. Clients want to be flattered."

"I prefer landscapes, but roses don't pay to have their image drawn."

He laughed at that, a deep rumble that resonated in my chest.

Frances perked up at the sound and turned our way. She gave me a narrow look, then put on a smile and flitted over to Treverton.

"I'm so glad to see you, my lord."

He motioned to the portrait. "I was just admiring your cousin's work."

She fluttered her fan. "I'm not sure it's the most flattering portrait I've ever had."

"Oh, it's quite flattering," he said.

I watched her try to decide if this was a compliment. Treverton was going to get me into trouble with the Medfords.

Finally, though, Frances shrugged it off. "I can't have you lingering out here. There are important people to talk to."

And with that, she tugged him away. She never gave me a backwards glance, but Treverton looked over his shoulder several times before Frances pulled him out of view.

I glowered at both of them. Frances was insufferable, and Treverton... What game was he playing? Trying to make me one of his flirts? He couldn't be serious. His grandfather would never allow him to pay his addresses to an orphaned refugee, a beggar and thief who dressed as a boy.

I forced myself to put on a content expression. This was

for Henri and for Beatrice. Neither Treverton nor I mattered to this scheme.

Beatrice had vanished somewhere. I skirted the edges of the guests, trying to pick up more gossip, but Mrs. Medford gave me a warning look. She didn't want me sullying the party. Hopefully, Beatrice heard something useful.

I retreated to the entrance hall. Mr. Hawke had started up the stairs toward the bedrooms. I raised an eyebrow. I would suspect him of seeking a dalliance, but he was alone, and the Medford girls were already in the ballroom with their guests.

"Mr. Hawke?" I asked. It wasn't my place, but this was my chance to question him.

He gave a guilty start, swallowing several times and making his Adam's apple jump erratically. "Cartier? Or, er, Carter? I'm, uh... I wanted to see... I got turned around."

"The party is that way." I pointed toward the obvious sound of people talking.

"Oh, yes, of course it is! Thank you."

He hurried past me for the ballroom, glancing several times back up the stairs.

"That was strange," Beatrice said at my elbow.

I jumped. "Yes. Very strange. Guilty, do you think?"

"He's guilty about something." Beatrice looked thoughtful. *"I never would have expected him to be a murderer."*

"But why would he sneak upstairs? He's been in this house before." Though, I remembered him giving the house searching looks on other occasions. Perhaps this was the first time he thought he could slip away unnoticed. "Do murderers really wish to revisit the scene of their crimes?"

"Heavens, I don't know. Maybe he was going to steal something?"

"A gentleman? Unlikely. But he wanted to look for something, I believe."

It could have to do with the Miss Medfords, but I struggled to see how. No, Hawke was hiding some guilty knowledge. We might have to frighten it out of him. But that would be difficult to do in the midst of a party which I could not attend.

I crept back to the ballroom. Hawke still lingered on the edge of the guests, fidgeting with his cravat. Beatrice followed him, apparently waiting for him to blurt out a confession.

Mrs. Medford had set Loretta to playing the pianoforte so Frances and the other young people could dance. I wanted to tell Treverton what I had found, but Frances had drawn him into her set. The dance brought them together, and she ran her fingers along his arm. He smirked down at her.

Watching them hit me like a blow to the chest. There was Frances, pouting and flirting her way to what she wanted, as always. The worst of it was knowing he was destined for her. I ought to have been concerned for her. After all, he was one of the possible murderers.

But I knew he wasn't the one. Not the one who had killed Beatrice. After what he had told me of his sister, I also knew he wasn't as heartless as he liked to pretend. No, he was the one I couldn't stop thinking about. Who made me feel warm and fluttery when I remembered his laugh or the keen way his green eyes watched me when we schemed together. As if he actually cared about what I thought and said.

Blast him.

I fled from the room, almost blindly. I made my way for the garden, a refuge where I only faintly heard the strains of the pianoforte. Where the cool, salt-laced air might clear my head.

I nearly ran down Beatrice's brother, who stood amid the poorly-pruned shrubbery, staring up at the house. I wondered if he had caught a glimpse of Beatrice.

"Mr. Foley?" I asked.

"Oh, uh, Carter, isn't it? The French aristocrat in exile? Forgive me. I found I could not join in the mood of the party. This house was my family's last season."

"Oh, I see. It must stir unpleasant memories."

"Not all unpleasant. Though, I almost expected my sister to come down those stairs, dressed in her silly parrot costume and apologizing for being late." He swallowed hard. "It still feels unreal that she is gone. I can't help wondering where I went wrong."

I thought of Henri with a guilty prickle. "I'm certain we all worry about younger siblings."

"Yes, they are a responsibility—even a burden at times —but they are still ours, and we must do all we can for them."

I didn't see Henri as a burden, but then I was not actually an older brother with career and future to think about. Perhaps it was different for men.

"Are your other family well?" I asked. "They are not here in Lymouth, are they?"

"No, Mother didn't wish to return, and I have my other sister settled in a good marriage. Beatrice could have made a good connection, too. Much better than Hawke, who was dangling after her."

"You didn't approve?"

"He wasn't good enough for my sister, and I told him so. Sent him packing. People thought she had run off with him at first, but she wouldn't have disobeyed me that way. She *wouldn't* have. I steered our ship with a firm hand, but she understood it was in her best interest."

He frowned at his hands, lost in his reminiscences.

Hawke wasn't good enough for Beatrice? Did Foley know something to the man's discredit? Hawke might have tried to lure Beatrice away, leading to her death, and now he felt guilty for it.

"You, uh, seem to be on polite terms with Hawke now," I said.

He shrugged one shoulder. "It's one thing to play cards with a man, and another to think of him as family. You must understand."

"Of course," I said, though I did not, and it was clear that Foley wasn't going to explain. I could only hope that Treverton had some insights when he was done flirting with the Miss Medfords.

I left Foley to his remembering and returned inside. Lord Martin was the last of my suspects. I'd caught a glimpse of him when he arrived—his invitation likely a result of Treverton's influence—and now he played cards with another gentleman in the corner.

Beatrice drifted over to me.

"Your brother is in the garden if you'd like to see him," I whispered.

"Are you going to talk to Lord Martin? I can help you win again if you want to play cards with him."

"What of your brother?"

"It's difficult, being able to see him but not speak to him."

I nodded my understanding. "I don't want to beat Lord Martin badly. My cousins will be upset if I fleece their guests."

"You ought to get something after all you do for them."

"Well, they are family."

"Then they should treat you like family as well!"

I frowned at that but had no response. How was family supposed to treat one? Like her brother had managed her? No one had ever guided me, with a firm hand or otherwise. My mother had been gentle and carefree, and then she was gone. Father may as well have been gone, too, consumed by his studies, leaving just Henri and me. The lack of guidance didn't make me free. Instead, it meant the burdens always fell on my shoulders. If family meant not feeling alone, then Beatrice was the closest to family I had.

I avoided Mrs. Medford and made my way to Lord Martin. He was already deep in his cups by the glazed look in his eyes.

"I'm not taking any more of your money," said the man he played against. "It's highway robbery when you're this foxed."

"Bah!" Martin said. "It's my money if I want to spend it!" His glassy gaze found me watching him. "You, Frenchman! You'll play me again, I'll wager."

Beatrice nodded eagerly.

I slid into a seat at his table. "I will play you, but only for shillings."

Beatrice frowned at me, but this felt more like robbery than snatching a bag of gold from someone's house, looking a man in the face and knowing he was not well and taking his money anyway. That was not who I wanted to be. If I sold a drawing or two in the next week, I'd have the money Henri needed without winning more of Lord Martin's.

"He could be drinking to drown his guilt," Beatrice reminded me. *"If he killed me, we ought to take every shilling he owns!"*

I scowled at that. If he was the killer, I would feel somewhat less guilty.

I took up my cards. "Have you danced tonight, Martin?"

"I don't fancy dancing. Or crowds."

"Then it's strange you came to a party."

He brayed his harsh laugh. "I knew there would be cards and wine, and it's a dangerous night to be about."

"How so?" I asked, ending the bidding as Beatrice urged.

"It's a cloudy night. Things will be afoot that we had all best not see."

My eyebrows rose at that. The smuggler's captain had said he had contacts in town, and such a person might do dangerous—deadly—things.

"Find out what he knows."

I dealt another round of cards. "Has anyone run afoul of these mysterious forces in the past?"

Martin swirled his wine and stared into the dark liquid. "The ocean keeps a multitude of secrets and holds the bones of many unfortunate men and women."

Beatrice leaned into his face. *"Do you know who killed me?*

Am I in the ocean?"

I pushed a shilling across the table. "Surely, no one in our circle has met such a fate, though."

"Funny thing about circles," he slurred, wrinkling his nose at his cards. "They all wind round and round and up and down until everyone is inside of them. Ugh, it makes me dizzy. I need another drink. When I stop drinking, I start thinking, and then I just feel...empty. I wonder what the point is of any of this. Eat, drink, and be merry, they say. So, I keep my cup filled."

I contemplated that as we finished our game. Lord Martin's forced, loud-mouthed gaiety struck me as hiding more sorrow than guilt. I might not think enough of my own amusement, but he thought far too much of his—and of nothing else.

Of course, he could be sorrowing over his contribution to Beatrice's death if she had seen something she shouldn't have. I won back my coins plus a few extra—but not too many. Still, I itched to count again and see how close I was to ten pounds.

As Lord Martin struggled to count out the cards for our next hand, a shriek sounded from the dancers.

I dropped the cards and swept up my coins before turning with everyone else to see what had happened.

"Ghost!" someone cried.

Beatrice and I exchanged confused looks. No one glanced in her direction.

"It's haunted!" Frances screamed, pointing at one of my sketches.

"Calm yourself, dear," Mrs. Medford said. "I'm sure it's

no such thing."

"But I saw the picture, and now it's changed. The girl who died last year, she appeared in it."

Everyone pressed closer to see.

"I'm sure your cousin did not intend for that," Mrs. Medford said. She noted me in the corner. "Charles, tell your cousin it's only a coincidence. This girl in the background is no one."

Everyone stared at me. Hawke, Foley, Treverton. Even poor bamboozled Martin. I could calm Frances down, tell her it was no one. But that wouldn't help Beatrice. And I was tired of helping Frances, especially as I saw her hanging on Treverton's arm.

I wrinkled my brow. "I'm sorry, madam. I don't know what to say. I did not add that figure to the painting."

Everyone stared at the picture. Beatrice drifted up to it and, puckering her lips in concentration, pushed the frame. The picture shifted on the wall as everyone watched.

Frances shrieked again and sank into Treverton's arms, though I caught the hint of a smile on her lips as she did so. Not what I had wanted to accomplish. But I forced myself to study the men.

Treverton paid little heed to Frances, instead meeting my eyes with a barely repressed smile. Martin merely looked perplexed and enjoyed a long swig of wine. Hawke had gone as pale as muslin and glanced around the room as though seeking an escape. How very interesting. Mrs. Medford might punish me later for not coddling Frances, but I had gained information about my suspects. If only I could pry Hawke's guilty secrets free.

CHAPTER 21

Frances lounged about the house the next day fanning herself and smiling like a fox who had raided a henhouse.

"Cousin Charles, did you see? The ball was a triumph!" she declared when I met my cousins in the yellow sitting room for lessons.

Even Loretta looked content for once as she worked on her embroidery, though she had been forced to play the pianoforte for Frances instead of dancing.

"You certainly made the most of the situation," Mrs. Medford agreed, giving me a dark look.

At least she couldn't blame me for making the picture move. Beatrice probably saved me with that trick.

"Everyone will talk about my party for ages. And those who weren't invited will be sorry they were not better acquainted with me." Frances's eyes gleamed. "Think, a ghost made an appearance!"

"The focus should have been on you," Mrs. Medford said. "And I still think someone played a prank on us."

"Oh, it doesn't matter," Frances said. "I had Lord Treverton's complete attention."

Ah, there was the cause of her unusually good mood.

Mrs. Medford softened. "Yes, you did very well, my dear."

"He was so easy to catch, I wonder if I am aiming too low. Perhaps Loretta should have him, and I can try for a marquess."

Loretta dropped her needle and scrambled after it on the floor.

"Well, one of you shall marry him," Mrs. Medford said. "That is certain."

It was all I could do not to flee the room and their horrible talk. As shallow as Treverton could be, he did not deserve to be treated like a prize to be won in a card game. And they only cared about his title and his wealth, just as he said. They were foolish not to appreciate the way his eyes sparkled when he tried not to laugh or the surprising sympathy beneath his mask of indifference.

Warmth spread through me at the thought, tingling over my cheeks.

I took a slow breath and released it. I could not indulge in such foolishness.

Perhaps Frances bothered me so because she played a game I could not participate in. After all, Treverton had to marry to please his grandfather, and I had nothing to offer.

As soon as I could manage, I escaped to the garden to create another sketch of Lymouth for the bookseller, drawing heavy clouds hanging low over the neat houses. I was only a couple of pounds short of freeing Henri. In a week, I would have my brother free, and we would start a new life away from Lymouth and my spoiled cousins. I never had to know how their little contest over Treverton ended.

"May I sit with you?"

Treverton's voice made me jump and smudge my drawing.

I eyed him warily. He didn't usually ask for anything he wanted—he simply claimed it. "It's more traditional to visit the ladies of the house after a party than their tutor."

"You're the most interesting lady in this house."

"Shh!" I reminded him.

He sighed and sat, though I had not told him he could. "I think we are safe in this garden. I have no wish to land you in trouble, though this masquerade grows tiresome."

A good reminder. I amused him for the moment, but he would eventually find me dull as he did everything else. I shuffled my shoe through the curled, brown leaves gathered by the bench.

"I hope you will at least tell me what you learned at the ball before you become bored with our pretense," I said.

"Oh, I will see this through, my friend, never fear. Miss Foley will be avenged."

"I didn't think you could be bothered to care about anyone," I said.

"For a time, I thought the same, but I'm beginning to remember my own heart."

He said it with a distant expression. Daydreaming about Frances? My stomach turned, and I crunched the leaves.

"I found Hawke trying to creep his way upstairs during the party," I said.

That brought his attention back to me. "Sneaking off to an assignation?"

"I had a sense it was even more scandalous. He acted guilty. Like he was looking for something. Something to do with Miss Foley, perhaps."

"He was one of her suitors. I never thought he had murder in him, but gentlemen in Society wear many masks."

"If he is the killer, how do we prove it?"

"We'd need something that tied him to Miss Foley's death. But you don't know how she died?"

I shook my head. "She doesn't remember." I reviewed what she had told me. "Oh! Her brooch! If we could find it, we would know who killed her."

"The killer might have sold it," Treverton said. "Of course, it was a unique piece, and that would have made it difficult to be rid of. He could still have it."

"Then how do we find out?"

He looked thoughtful, then grinned. "Do you still fancy climbing into a gentleman's window?"

"What?" I asked.

"You seemed to be considering it when I first encountered you, and that's the easiest way to find answers: check his chambers while he's distracted."

"How much danger is involved if we're caught?"

"Oh, for the person doing the climbing, a great deal."

"And you'll pretend to be shocked and help haul me off to the magistrate?"

He laughed. "I'm not ready to give up our game so soon; I'll keep Hawke off your scent. Are you willing to try?"

His eyes sparkled, and a matching excitement stirred in my chest. We could find answers for Beatrice, and my heart-beat quickened at the thought of outwitting Hawke if he was the killer.

But I could not be arrested or lose my position—not with less than a week until Henri returned and I freed him. After that, I could take more risks.

No, after that, I would be gone.

I looked down at my half-finished sketch. "I'll think on it."

He sat in silence for a moment. "Very well."

I didn't want to see his disappointment, but it laced his words, and I cringed inwardly. Saving Henri was all that mattered in the end. But I had not anticipated the weight of the cost.

He stood. "I suppose I ought to call on your cousins, then. Good day."

I waited until his footsteps faded, then closed my sketch-book and walked back inside, trying to restore my carefree, boyish façade. Treverton was threatening my disguise, and I could not allow that.

Loretta sat at the pianoforte in the ballroom, playing a sad song, a stark contrast to the cheerful dance tunes of the night before.

"Bonjour, Cousin Loretta," I said.

She turned. "Oh, Cousin Charles. I'm afraid I am not much in the mood for French today. Please, let's not speak it."

I wanted to ask what she thought people in France did when they were not in the mood for French, but I could see she was honestly upset.

I sat in the chair by the instrument. "Would you like to tell me about it? In English?"

"Oh, you are very kind! No one in this house ever wants to listen to me. I hope it will not seem rude, but sometimes I could imagine you were a lady. I don't mean..." She pinked and looked down at the instrument. "I admit, at first, I did not trust you, but only a true cousin would tolerate all that we have asked of you. And you are gentler than most men. Perhaps that is the way of the French."

It most certainly was not, which she would know if she had seen France lately, but I didn't tell her so. "I am a good listener, at least."

"I'm glad. A male perspective might help. You see, the reason I don't want to speak French is that it's supposed to be the language of love."

Beatrice drifted into the room, looking curious.

"Oh?" I asked.

Loretta sighed. "My heart is entangled, but I do not think Mother will approve. She has plans for us, you know. Mostly for Frances, but I am to do whatever Frances does not wish to."

"And her plans are—" I stopped myself. I already knew, and I did not want to hear it.

"Lord Treverton, of course," Loretta said. "Mother wants him for Frances, but Frances isn't sure if he's good enough for her. If she does not want him, I will have to marry him."

I felt ill at the thought, but that was ridiculous. Treverton's grandfather demanded that he marry, and my cousins were just the right sorts—proper young ladies with dowries and a good name. They had never stolen or begged or slept in the dirt. Nor had they ever schemed with Treverton about how to break into the chambers of a possible murderer.

"There is someone you would rather marry?" I choked out.

Her face softened. "Oh, yes. I am in love with Geoffrey Hawke."

"Mr. Hawke!" Cold seeped over me.

Beatrice shook her head. *"Bad idea!"*

Loretta looked concerned at my outburst. "Is he not a good man?"

"I, uh, don't know him well. It's always wise for a young woman to be cautious, though."

"I have been cautious. I am always cautious," she said with a bitter edge. "I've had to disguise my feelings from everyone. Except Mr. Hawke. We love each other, but as long as Lord Treverton is around, Mama won't even consider a younger son like Mr. Hawke."

Was he sneaking off to see her at the ball, then? But she had been in the ballroom. No, his behavior still made no sense. "You know him well? You trust him?"

She smiled, her expression dreamy. "Oh, yes; I feel as though our souls are entwined. He thought he was in love once before, but he tells me he didn't know his heart then, and what we have now is more lasting."

"Well!" Beatrice folded her arms. *"And men say women are fickle."*

"Hmm," I replied to both of them.

Was Hawke the kind of man who would murder a girl to get out of a relationship he didn't want? Or did Beatrice refuse him, and so he killed her in a fit of rage?

"But my only hope is if Lord Treverton marries Frances or passes me over," Loretta said. "Will he, do you think?"

"I don't know," I mumbled. "He does not speak to me of such things."

"At least that means he is gentlemanly. Sometimes he confuses me. He looks like he is always laughing at something I don't understand, and I'm afraid it is me that he is laughing at."

"He is not a...a comfortable man, but I don't think he would be a cruel husband." In fact, when he put aside his arrogant demeanor, he could be charming and amusing. Even a sympathetic friend at times.

But I would never know. And I couldn't allow myself to mourn him. If he was foolish enough to bestow his humor and affections on someone that didn't understand them, then he deserved the empty life he chose. Poor Loretta didn't deserve it, but I struggled to find a way to help her with her mother.

One thing I could help her with was Hawke. If he was a murderer, I had to unmask him before he could lure in Loretta or anyone else.

Voices from the entrance hall signaled the arrival of visitors. Treverton.

Loretta sighed and stood, straightening her dress. I followed her out of the room. My heart caught at the sight of Treverton bowing to Frances in the drawing room.

He met my eyes, his gaze curious.

I nodded once, decisively.

His eyebrows rose, and then he smiled in understanding. We would be breaking into Mr. Hawke's chambers.

CHAPTER 22

Treverton slipped me a note, instructing me to meet him on Lymouth's high street an hour after sunset.

Easily enough done. I snuck out of the Medford's house that evening as they listened to Frances practice the pianoforte. Beatrice glided along beside me.

"You're helping me, after all. Maybe I can help you."

Guilt shot through me. I had been willing to put this off at least until after I rescued Henri. "Thank you."

When I passed the bookshop displaying my sketches of Lymouth, nervous flutters erupted in my stomach.

"They look lovely."

"I hope many people think so," I said.

Then I continued past the white-washed buildings to find Lord Treverton waiting for me in a shadowed alley. Beatrice lingered in the street, keeping watch, while I went to meet him.

"I'm glad you decided to do this after all," he said, stepping close enough that his scent of orange water enveloped me. "You need to enjoy life more."

I folded my arms. I didn't want to admit the thrill coursing through my veins. "You think this will be enjoyable?"

He grinned. "Yes. An adventure."

I dropped my gaze to the hard-packed ground of the alley. "I'm doing this to help Beatrice and Loretta. To make certain Hawke doesn't hurt anyone."

His forehead creased. "Don't you ever do *anything* because you want to?"

"I *want* to help them."

He took another step nearer, so close I could feel his warmth. He brushed a stray lock from my forehead, sending a pleasant shiver through me. "But what about helping yourself?" he asked, his voice low.

I met his eyes and couldn't look away from the concern —and something else—reflected in them. His gaze traced my face, coming to rest on my lips. His fingers reached tentatively for my arm, drawing a searing trail through my sleeve down to my hand. My lips parted, and I leaned forward.

No.

I was not just some amusing distraction for Lord Treverton. And I wasn't allowed distractions for myself.

I clenched my hand, breaking from his touch, and swallowed twice before I found my voice. "I—I can't think of myself. Not when others rely on me."

He huffed. "Others rely on me, and yet when I don't do everything for them, they muddle on somehow."

"Yes, you are very good at thinking about yourself," I snapped. "I am not a—a cad!"

I winced. He was helping me after all, and I should not have lost my temper with him.

But he laughed. "I should hope not."

I grumbled and stalked back along high street, dodging the puddles of light that escaped from cracks in curtained windows. He kept pace with me, a secretive little smile quirking one corner of his lips.

"What is your plan then?" I finally asked.

"While I am visiting Hawke, I will pretend to find a rat and throw it out the bedroom window, leaving it cracked open. Then I will keep him occupied in the drawing room while you sneak in."

"And if he catches me?"

"You could pretend to be deranged," Treverton said with a wicked grin.

I rolled my eyes. I couldn't count on Treverton. I would just have to avoid being caught.

I waited outside while he went in for his appointed meeting with Hawke.

"*He's a bit rakish,*" Beatrice said thoughtfully, "*but not entirely wrong.*"

I jumped and whispered, "What do you mean?"

"*Well, he should not come so close to kissing you. Not in public. It could have ruined both of you...*"

My cheeks burned, and I was tempted to cover them with my chilly hands. "It would have ruined me for certain. And I suppose it would not look well for him, kissing a French tutor in the street."

Beatrice giggled. *"Not at all! He could have revealed you as a girl, but then he would have to marry you."*

My breath caught. "What?"

"You're an orphan without a dowry, but you're still a young lady from a good family. And I don't think he's forgotten that."

"I'm certain he has." I shoved my hands into the pockets of my trousers. Who would ever think me a gently-born young lady now?

"Hmm. Regardless, I agree with him. I've never seen you do anything for own well-being."

I shrugged. "I've been otherwise occupied."

"Oh, I don't mean to sound ungrateful. Quite the opposite. I know I was quite a silly girl, and I don't know that being dead has made me less foolish, but it seems unwise to never take a few moments for yourself. My mother was a good, doting mama, but she still liked to spend time with a novel. And my brother managed everything after our father died but still found plenty of time for his friends."

I hunched my shoulders. "Perhaps. But it's different for me."

"I know you don't have the financial luxury at the moment—"

I shook my head. "It's not only that. It's..." I paused. How did I explain it to her? That this was all I'd ever known? All I'd ever been? I didn't know *how* to be anything but helpful and useful, and it frightened me.

A commotion from inside saved me from finding the words. The window overhead slid open.

"I'll toss it out into the street," Treverton called.

He leaned out and gave me a wink, then he pulled inside, leaving the window cracked.

My cue. I drew a deep breath and climbed the trellis screwed into the brick front of the building. Beatrice hovered below me.

"Be careful! Don't look down!"

I huffed and kept my eyes firmly on the window ahead of me, not wanting to think about falling. I trusted Beatrice to warn me if anyone approached.

When I pulled myself carefully through the window, Beatrice reappeared in the bedroom.

She drifted around the chamber, examining the neatly made bed and the clothes press and large trunks lined up along one wall. *"Oh, this is exciting! Do you think we'll find the brooch?"*

I shrugged, not willing to even whisper. Not when I had finally resorted to trespassing and perhaps even robbery. I shuffled through Hawke's closet and trunks. His clothes were all clean and pressed, the few books on practical topics like agriculture. He kept letters from sisters, but none that seemed to be from mistresses or criminal counterparts. Nothing scandalous, nothing telling. A little dull.

"I suppose he would have made a safe husband after all," Beatrice said. *"Oh, look! He has one of your drawings."*

My heart jumped, and I found my drawing of the bronze angel on the wall. A flash of pleasure mingled with regret shot through me. I had secretly hoped that no one would purchase her. But I had made a little more money for Henri. And—I had to admit—I was pleased on my own account that someone had thought my sketches worth buying.

Beatrice swung around, passing right through the shaving basin balanced on the edge of the dressing table. It crashed to the floor with a horrible clank.

I stared in horror.

"I did that!" Beatrice said. *"I think I'm getting better at haunting. Did you see?"*

I saw that I needed to escape quickly.

"It was probably another rat." Treverton's voice was too loud, coming from the corridor.

I threw myself into one of the open trunks and buried myself among Hawke's linen shirts.

"Your foot!" Beatrice warned.

I wiggled it down.

"Good!"

The door clicked open.

"Oh, it was my shaving basin. Everything else looks undisturbed. Good heavens, I hope it wasn't a rat that knocked it down."

"Try to breathe less."

I held my breath, letting it out very slowly.

"Unless you have a ghost," Treverton said lightly. "Not haunted, are you?"

"Ha!" Hawke said. "I know you're joking, but sometimes I wonder..."

"Oh?" Treverton asked. "Something from your past catching up with you?"

"I'll keep my own councils, thank you."

"We all have some skeletons in our closets," Treverton said. "Might not be so troubled by it if you got it off your chest. Unless it's too scandalous. Some secret sin."

"Wouldn't you like that? Nothing so gothic, I assure you. I have only wondered… You recall Miss Foley last year."

I took a slow breath and held it.

"Oh, vaguely." Treverton sounded bored.

"I was quite fond of her," he said. "I sometimes wonder if I was one of the last people to see her before she vanished."

"Catch her eloping with another fellow, did you?"

"Not at all! I went to her garden after the costume ball. She left early, and I wanted another glimpse of her. I had hoped to convince her family to let me court her, though her brother never thought I was wealthy enough."

"And you found her sneaking out of the house with a bandbox?"

"Don't be ridiculous. She waved at me from the window and motioned as if she would come down."

"Oh?" A little of Treverton's curiosity slipped through now.

"She never appeared. Maybe I misunderstood her intentions. I waited for a while, until I heard voices approaching the garden, and then I hurried away so I wouldn't get caught and cause her scandal. And I never saw her again. I often wonder what became of her."

I let out my breath and slowly sucked in another. A shirt-sleeve stuck to my nose.

"You were sneaking around her old house at the Medfords' party." Treverton's voice had a sharp edge.

"How did you—" Hawke huffed. "Blast it. Yes, I was. I thought maybe I could find some hint about her fate. Silly of me, since everyone had already searched."

"That is hardly a dramatic confession," Treverton said. "Can't you do any better?"

"We don't all wrack up a train of devils behind us like you do."

"Speaking of which, this isn't exactly the evening you promised. Shall we return to our cards?"

They exited the room. After a long pause, I emerged from my burial among the clothes and hurried for the window.

"*Did you hear that?*" Beatrice asked. "*What do you think it means?*"

I didn't dare answer. I scurried out the window and climbed down as quickly as I dared.

"*Well?*" Beatrice asked as soon as I reached the ground.

I jumped. "I wish you wouldn't sneak up on me."

"*Oh, I apologize, but you heard all of that, didn't you?*"

"I heard that Hawke saw you from the window, but then you didn't come down. It fits with what you remember."

"*Do you think he was telling the truth?*"

"Well, he didn't have the brooch." I said, hurrying toward the Medford's house. "So, assuming he's telling the truth, either something prevented you from going down to see him, or..."

"*Or?*" Beatrice asked breathlessly.

"Or...he mentioned hearing other voices near the garden. What if you went down after he left and ran into someone else? Someone who killed you."

"Stop right there," a cold, male voice said.

"*Oh, dear!*"

I froze. What to do in a smuggling town? Turn to face the wall.

"None of that," the man said. "I want to see your face."

I spun slowly to see my captor: the sharp-eyed man from the bookshop—the one who thought I was a spy.

"I remember you," he said. "The French lad. What are you doing out so late?"

It was dangerous to lie to a revenue man, which he probably was, so I chose my words carefully. "I was visiting friends, sir."

He stepped closer and took a deep breath. "You don't smell of wine, but you were talking to yourself."

Beatrice covered her mouth. *"I'm sorry! I should have seen him."*

"I was...was trying to work out a story."

"About murder?"

I shrugged a shoulder. "It makes for an interesting novel, don't you think?"

"I don't read novels."

Of course not. "Ah. Then you would not want to discuss it. If I'm free to go?"

"I believe I should see you home. You are young, and there may be dangerous people about."

I bowed my assent, trying to act as casual as possible. Beatrice drifted behind us, wringing her hands.

I approached the Medfords' house through the garden, wondering if some other figure had lurked in the garden the night of Beatrice's death. My not-so-friendly escort stayed on my heels like the hounds of death.

I turned to him when I reached the garden door. "Thank you for seeing to my safety, sir."

The door swung open, and Mrs. Medford loomed over us.

"Charles! What are you doing out so late, and who is this person?"

"You know this young man?" the revenue man asked her.

Mrs. Medford straightened and peered down her nose at him, despite the fact that he was several inches taller. "I do not believe we have been properly introduced."

I wanted to applaud my cousin's ability to cut. Even the revenue man quelled a little under her frosty stare.

"Forgive me, cousin," I said. "I do not know this person to offer you an introduction. He claimed he wished to see me safely home, on account of my youth and my newness in England."

Mrs. Medford narrowed her eyes at the man. "Very well. You have done your duty, and you may go."

The revenue man looked like he wished to argue, but since he had no cause to accuse me or my cousins, he bowed and strode off into the night.

"Now," Mrs. Medford said, turning that icy gaze on me and dragging me inside, "you will explain what you have been doing that ends in you bringing low men to my back door in the middle of the night."

She shut the door behind me.

I hung my head. "I was playing cards with some other men. Men who have been to France and remind me of home." When had lying become so second nature to me?

"I see. I can understand your desire for masculine company, but I will not tolerate you giving this household a reputation for inmates coming and going at all hours, and I never want to see a revenue man at my door again."

"Yes, madam," I said quickly. "I will not be out so late again."

"Was Lord Treverton there?" she asked.

"Yes?" I responded, not sure if that was wise.

"Did he say anything about my girls?"

I drew myself up. "No, madam! It would be ungentlemanly to discuss young ladies at a card party."

She looked disappointed. Wrong answer.

"Don't let me catch you sneaking out again, or you will be dismissed."

I bowed my head and hurried past her.

At the top of the stairs, Frances stood, watching the whole scene. She regarded me with a dangerous gleam in her eyes. My stomach tightened. I didn't understand what she wanted from me, but I feared she would have it.

And I would likely have to be out late again, because we still didn't know who had killed Beatrice.

CHAPTER 23

I could feel Mrs. Medford watching me the next day, pinning me in the house. And there was no sign of Beatrice, which worried me. Had she gone out on her own? I itched to gather whatever funds the bookshop had for Henri, and to ask Treverton what he thought of Hawke. Yet between Mrs. Medford and the suspicious revenue man lurking out there, I was trapped inside with Frances, who regarded me with keen, malicious eyes.

As I worked on a sketch of Paris in the throes of the Revolution, Frances reclined on the sofa and studied me.

"Treverton has taken a liking to you," she said.

I shrugged one shoulder. "I'm not so certain. He's a difficult man to read."

"Yet as a male, you have an advantage, do you not? You can go where a female would not. It seems so unfair."

"That may be true, though the goals of male and female acquaintances are likely to be vastly different."

"Then what is your goal?" She leaned forward and lowered her voice as though sharing a secret. "Tell me why you seek his company."

I paused my sketching and looked up into her gaze—as sharp as a needle. What did she expect me to say? "It is pleasant to have someone to talk to who knows... where I come from."

"Hmm." She lifted her fan, flicking it open and closed. "I imagine you also want to attach yourself to someone who can offer you a future. An earl can keep any number of people around who amuse him. Court jesters, if you will. Even people who fancy themselves artists."

Of course, she would see it that way—that I was only using Treverton. That I could not succeed on my own. I remembered that Hawke had purchased one of my drawings and hung it on his wall. And given what I had seen of Frances, she had no eye for art. I made no reply.

Frances went on, "I only worry for you, that he'll soon find you tiresome. He grows bored easily."

I pressed my lips together. I knew that well enough; I constantly reminded myself of it. "Then don't you worry he'll grow bored of you as well?"

Something flashed in her eyes: desperate fear, hardening to rage. "I am much more charming and witty than other young ladies, which you would realize if you knew anything." Her expression cooled. "And as long as he doesn't grow bored until after I'm a countess, what do I care? At least I will be comfortable again, never to fear being poor as we have been since Father died." She cast me a sly look. "And I will not forget those who help me achieve success. Those who put a kind word in Treverton's ear. Or those who oppose me."

I wanted to tell her that she was no more charming than a shrieking fishwife on the streets of Paris. That I would never say a kind word to Treverton about her. But I only returned to my drawing with renewed energy, adding to the swirling chaos of the image of revolution.

Mrs. Medford marched into the room and smiled upon her indolent offspring. "I have excellent news. Lord Treverton will be joining us for dinner in a couple of nights. An intimate occasion with just a few friends."

My heart picked up its pace. He was coming to see my cousins, of course, but at least I would have a chance to ask him about Hawke. And in the confusion of preparations, I could sneak down to the bookshop.

But Mrs. Medford turned her gaze on me. "I will have you scrub the dining room, Charles."

"Me?" I asked.

"Of course. Everyone will have to work together to make the evening a success, especially in such a short time. You do want your cousins to succeed, don't you?"

Frances smirked at me.

I lowered my eyes to the bloody scene on my paper. Did I wish them to succeed? Loretta, perhaps, since Hawke did not appear to be a danger to her. But I didn't wish for Frances's success. I imagined her in a tumbrel headed to the guillotine but blinked the image away. No, I didn't wish that on anyone. But I also didn't want to imagine her in Treverton's arms. I would have to be far from the dining room when Treverton visited. I could not stomach watching him court either of my cousins—Frances who enjoyed it, and Loretta who did not.

I took up my sketchbook and marched off to the dining room where a bucket and pile of rags awaited me. I did a quick sketch of myself scrubbing the floor while Mrs. Medford stood on my back. There was an image no one wanted to purchase, but I felt a bit better for having drawn it. I snapped the book shut and rolled up my sleeves to clean.

"I found you!" Beatrice appeared in front of me as I knelt on the hard wooden planks. *"What are they making you do now?"*

"Making sure the floor shines for when Lord Treverton comes to dinner," I mumbled. Was this how Henri spent his days—scrubbing decks?

"Oh, their audacity! But you'll turn that on their heads."

"How so?"

She put her hands on her hips. *"It cannot have escaped your notice that Treverton's attentions are fixed on you, not them."*

I sighed and wiped my forehead. "Only because I amuse him. Even a man like him cannot marry simply for amusement."

"I believe he will do what pleases him best."

But he had to please his grandfather. I thrust a rag in the bucket and plopped the sopping mess on the floor to scrub. "Have you been out investigating this morning?"

Her forehead wrinkled. *"No. I don't think so. I don't know where I was. But I have a sense it was dark."*

My stomach tightened, and I sat back to study her. Did

she look less solid than before? "Maybe being away from the house and tipping over that shaving basin exhausted you."

"Maybe." She stared at something off in the distance. *"The dark frightens me. I am afraid it will swallow me completely someday. Yet other times I feel this incredible sense of light and peace just out of reach. If I only can touch it."*

"I'm afraid I'm failing you," I said quietly. "But we won't let the darkness take you."

She shuddered, then she focused on me again. *"I have had enough of darkness. Let us speak of light. Tell me of...of places that you have visited so I can imagine I have seen them, too."*

Images of revolution and bloodshed flashed through my mind, but those would not help Beatrice. I forced those memories away. I had never done a Grand Tour, but Father, Henri, and I had traveled through France for his studies, so I told Beatrice about ancient forests and snow-blanketed mountains.

"Charles?" Loretta called from the corridor.

Beatrice's eyes went wide, and I halted my rambling.

"Who are you talking to?" Loretta asked. She stopped when she saw me kneeling on the floor. "They have you scrubbing now?"

I nodded.

She sighed and knelt beside me. "Hand me a rag."

I stared at her. "I think you'd better not. Your mother will be furious."

Her shoulders sagged. "She won't even notice."

I hesitated, but Loretta's face was determined. She held out a hand, and I passed her a rag.

"What were you muttering about when I came in?" she asked.

"Just remembering happier times."

She frowned and scraped at a stain on the floor with her fingernail. "Those sometimes seem so far away. I feel trapped here, missing Father, not even permitted to mourn without upsetting... Well. I'm the one who must always be quiet and good. I have to leave the emotions to other people in my family. Would you share one of your happier times with me?"

I was wary of telling her more about myself, but I ached at her loneliness, so much like my own. "Of course. We can cheer each other as we work."

Before long, the floor shone, and Loretta and I shared stories of our childhood while Beatrice listened in rapt fascination. For that short time, the darkness stayed away.

CHAPTER 24

The next morning found me working alone since Loretta was forced to spend much of the day preparing for dinner with Treverton and Beatrice had failed to appear again. Worry over her knotted my stomach, but Mrs. Medford kept me too busy to escape the house and search for answers.

"Oh, Charles," Frances said, bouncing into the sitting room where I shoved a sofa aside so the chambermaid could sweep behind it. "I know you have helped prepare for this dinner party, and you must hope to attend, but mother is counting on you being absent. If you were included, the numbers would be uneven, you see."

"Of course, I understand," I said. I had not expected to be invited.

Frances smirked and swished back to the preparations. Had she only wished to remind me that I was not wanted? I was relieved that the Medfords would not be looking for me during dinner, but it still rankled that they excluded me so easily.

When the guests arrived, I hid in the attic. Beatrice appeared, looking fainter than usual. I wondered if all our activity harmed her.

"Perhaps you should stay in here and rest," I said.

She shook her head. *"You don't understand. Before you arrived, it was always like this. I often faded away. Having someone to talk to brought me back, but I don't think it can last. For now, I want to go down to the dinner. I wonder what they are eating?"*

She left me to spy on the party below, but she returned shortly, looking disgusted.

"I hope I never acted that...that stupid when a man was courting me!"

I chuckled, but my stomach soured. Treverton would get what he deserved for chasing the Medfords. Or his grandfather would.

"Is the way clear for me to sneak out?" I asked. "I want to see if the bookseller has any money for Henri."

Beatrice assured me that it was—even the servants were too busy with the dinner to pay any attention to me.

I hurried out and made my way to the bookseller's. He was just closing up for the night.

"Oh, I do have some sales for you," he said. "I hope you have more drawings? They are very popular with the ladies, especially when they learn they were painted by an émigré."

"Oh, wonderful," I said drily. They wouldn't be so happy if they knew they were painted by a woman masquerading as a man.

He counted out my coins, and I took them carefully, trying to keep my fingers from trembling. I had done the arithmetic. I was only a few shillings shy of the amount I needed to save Henri. I practically skipped my way home.

Beatrice met me at the back door, wringing her hands. *"I am glad you've returned. You had better stop Lord Treverton."*

"Stop him?" I whispered. "What is he doing?"

If he was proposing to Frances, there was little I could do. I clutched the coins in my pocket.

"He appears to be drunk. And he wandered away from the party looking for you. He...he asked me to find you, though I'm not certain he actually knew I was watching."

Impossible man! He was going to give me away. I hurried down the corridor and found him staring wistfully at a rather bad landscape painting.

"You should not be wandering about." I scolded. "You are drunk!"

"Nonsense, my lady." He glared at me steadily, but with eyes a little too bright. "Only a trifle disguised."

I looked about to be sure no one was watching, then grabbed his arm and marched him behind a heavy curtain sheltering a window alcove.

"Have you lost your senses?" I asked.

"You know," he said slowly, giving me a very odd once over. "I'm rather afraid I have."

"For heaven's sake. This is no time to fall into a mad streak. You are supposed to be courting my cousins, and there may be a killer wandering Lymouth. We have to keep our heads."

He stared off over my shoulder, his expression glazed,

but then he blinked and looked back to me. "You are right, I suppose. I should have kept my head. But you weren't at the dinner, and you were the only one I wanted to see. I had to find you."

"Oh, I suppose you were bored with Frances and poor Loretta."

"I wasn't paying any attention to them. I couldn't stop thinking about you."

"You'll become bored of me just as you did them," I said.

He shook his head. "I didn't become bored with them; they were always tiresome. But not you. I would not tire of you if I saw you every day for the rest of our lives. A very pleasant idea, I find."

That stopped the trail of my thoughts. He couldn't possibly mean what it sounded like he meant. He was an English heir to an earldom, and I was an orphaned French refugee.

"You shouldn't be thinking of me," I said, my voice tight.

"Oh, shouldn't I?" He leaned closer and gently rested a hand on my arm, sending a flood of warmth through me. "I can think of whomever I like. Who will gainsay me?"

I pulled my arm away. "Your behavior is...is unworthy!"

"Unworthy? I? But I am Lord Treverton."

"Exactly. You march into Lymouth and everyone bows and simpers to your every word. They pile their daughters at your feet, and you walk over them like they are so many stones on the street."

"Do I? Well, I suppose I have become rather used to them throwing themselves at me."

"You are toying with them. With all the young ladies, and

my cousins in particular. You should leave the Medfords alone. Especially Miss Loretta."

"I thought you liked Miss Loretta."

"I do. That is why you should leave her alone."

"Her mama seems to think I should be an excellent catch for her."

"But what have you ever done to deserve a sweet girl?"

"I suppose I am not very sweet-tempered myself." He frowned. "Do you think I would be a beastly husband, then?"

I caught glimpses in him of a man who would make a charming and entertaining husband—even a kind one. One I could imagine sharing my days with, if I dared to dream. But his self-importance kept stepping in the way.

"I think you are spoiled and selfish," I choked out.

"Probably true. But it doesn't matter as long as I have the promise of money and a title." His voice held a bitter edge. "I can make some fortunate lady a countess, you know."

I folded my arms. "Only a fool marries a title. And only a fool would want to marry a girl who only cared about being a countess." My voice caught, and my face flushed hot. "You ought to aim for something better, and then be deserving of it. You expect everyone's devotion as your due, but you do not earn it—all you did was to be born and then you expect the world to tumble at your feet."

"And yet, the one woman I would like to see swoon over me won't do it."

He grabbed my hand and pulled me closer. His scent of oranges washed over me, and I felt lightheaded at his nearness.

I wanted to scream at him that it wasn't fair. He wasn't

allowed to make me fall in love with him while he courted someone else. All I managed was a shaky, "I don't belong to you."

"Alas, I know it. And yet, I begin to think that I belong to you. You are remarkable, and I wish I could make you see it."

I gaped at him. He was too drunk to think clearly. Otherwise, he would not say such things. His grandfather would never allow him to marry someone like me—if he even thought of marriage and not a flirtation. But he looked at me with such intensity, I couldn't find the words to tell him so. I could only stare. And when his gaze focused on my mouth, and he leaned forward, I matched his movement.

His lips met mine softly. His grip on my hand slackened, and he traced his fingers down to my elbow and then up my back. I leaned into the kiss, totally lost in the warmth of his body so close to mine.

"*Charlotte!*" a voice hissed from very far away.

"Mmm?" I asked, not breaking off the kiss.

Treverton made a questioning noise back and deepened the kiss.

"*Charlotte, someone is coming!*" It was Beatrice.

And behind her, the merry voices of the dinner party.

I gave a start and broke from Treverton. "They are coming!"

He looked horrified and whispered, "No one can see us together."

His words hit me like a slap. Of course, I had been thinking it, but to hear it from him like that made me ill. He was destined to marry one of the Miss Medfords, but he knew that no one cared about me and he could trifle with me without consequence.

"Never fear!" I hissed. "No one ever will."

I gave him a shove, sending him out of the alcove alone. I huddled against the dark window, blinking back tears. The happy voices swarmed Treverton, carried him away to some game of cards or a performance on the pianoforte. Their words swam around me, making no sense. None of the happiness was for me. As soon as the way was clear, I fled for the attic.

CHAPTER 25

I kept myself locked away in the attic that night and into the next day, determined to avoid my cousins and everything about the house.

"What do you plan to do next?" Beatrice asked when she finally appeared again.

"I don't know. I'm so close to saving Henri, and then I can leave." I looked up at her. "I don't know how to find your killer. If it's not Hawke, I would guess it's Lord Martin. He's mentioned knowing things about the smugglers, but I don't know how to prove it."

Her eyes brightened. *"What if I helped you break into his house? You could find my brooch and prove he was the one who killed me. And he probably has a few shillings you could steal."*

"Really?" I asked. "You would help me steal?"

"From my killer? Of course!"

I didn't want to steal anything else—especially if Lord

Martin turned out to be innocent. But the moon had nearly vanished from the sky. I was out of time. "Very well."

I peeked out to make sure no one was watching then hurried down the stairs, heading for the back door.

"Charles!" Mrs. Medford's voice caught me. "Where are you going?"

Beatrice disappeared at the sound of her voice.

I gritted my teeth, then put on an innocent expression. "The...the garden."

"Well, if you have time to lounge about the garden, you have time to work. We'll be throwing an engagement ball soon, and we must all help make the house look its best."

The words came like a kick to my chest. I had to fight not to wrap my arms around myself.

"Did Lord Treverton propose, then?" I mumbled.

She scowled. "Not yet, but he must any day now. I happen to know he has been exchanging letters with his grandfather the earl, and that can only mean he is making arrangements. So, you will start in the entrance hall and work your way up the stairs. Remove the carpets and beat them."

I wanted to scream at her. But that would guarantee I was thrown out, and probably beaten myself in the process. And I was so close to freeing Henri and escaping Lymouth forever.

Instead of protesting, I rolled up the entrance rug and hauled it outside, then I pulled up the rods holding the stair carpet in place. I doubted the rug had been moved in ages, based on the dust and dirt jammed under the rods.

I rolled the carpet down the stairs, coughing at the dust

kicked up by the rug. Mrs. Medford would probably make me scrub the stairs, too, if the chambermaid was too busy.

Something on one of the top steps caught my eye. A little brooch shaped like a bird and set with emeralds. It had been hidden under the rug.

A chill raced over my skin, and I picked up the brooch.

"Beatrice?" I whispered.

Nothing.

"Beatrice!"

She appeared next to me.

Her eyes widened, and she reached a trembling hand toward the brooch. *"That's it! That's my mother's brooch. Where did you find it?"*

"On the stairs. Under the carpet. It's been here a long time..."

"It's been here since I died. It never left the house." She clutched her chest. *"I never left the house."*

We stared at one another.

"Someone in my household did this to me?" Her voice rose to a high pitch.

I nodded slowly and stared at the brooch. "And they weren't trying to rob you or they would not have left this behind."

"What do we do with this?" Beatrice asked.

"I'll hold onto it."

"What are you holding on to?" Frances asked from the top landing. "What do you have there?"

I shoved my hands in my pockets, but Frances was quick. She grabbed my hand and pulled it free, spilling the brooch out with it.

194 • E.B. WHEELER

"You found this?" Her eyes narrowed. "You were going to keep it."

"I was going to find its proper owner."

"Well, it's mine," Frances said, tugging at it. "I lost it."

"It's not!" I said.

Beatrice tried to pound Frances's back, but it did nothing.

Frances glared at me. "I am to be a countess someday. You should not cross me."

I yanked the brooch away, and Frances tumbled to the ground.

Her face turned bright red, and she glared at me with pure hate. "Mother! Charles is robbing us!"

That brought everyone in the household running to gawk. I was trapped, with Frances and the maids at the top of the stairs and Mrs. Medford and Loretta at the bottom. I glared at Frances, holding the brooch just out of her reach.

"Give that to me!" Mrs. Medford demanded.

"It's not hers," I said. "It belonged to Miss Foley."

"Nonsense!" Mrs. Medford said. "Give it to me."

I clutched the brooch until the metal bit into my palm. "You know your daughter is lying! You know, and you let her do it anyway. You're not helping her. You're making it worse. You're making her an unbearable brat!"

And I had played along for far too long, trying to please and placate her.

"Monster!" Frances wailed. "He's probably been stealing from us this whole time. Maybe he's not even our cousin. He came here to rob us!"

Mrs. Medford wrenched the brooch from my fingers and

shoved it into the pocket in her skirts. Then she grabbed my arm and marched me up the stairs.

"We'll examine your room and see what else you're hiding," she said.

She threw me onto the floor of the attic and proceeded to turn out the trunks and chests. Frances watched with delight, and Loretta stared with huge, frightened eyes.

Mrs. Medford turned over my mattress, and her eyes fixed on my coin purse.

"What do you have here?" she snatched it up and weighed it with glee. "You been stealing coins, I see."

"No!" The word came out hot and raw. I scrambled to my feet and lunged after the coin purse. "That is mine. It's for my brother. I won't let you take it."

Her backhanded slap sent me reeling.

"What's that?" Frances pounced on the one red slipper left from my night at the masquerade. I had been a fool to keep it.

Mrs. Medford lifted it.

"This is the slipper that mystery girl wore." Frances's eyes narrowed. "She was French, too. You are in league with her."

"No doubt robbing the wealthy families of Lymouth," Mrs. Medford said.

"No, I didn't! That was Miss Foley's dress. She lived here. She died here! We have to tell someone."

"I've heard enough from you," Mrs. Medford said. "I'll keep you locked in here until I've decided how to deal with this without creating a scandal for my girls."

I scrambled for the door, for escape, but Mrs. Medford

smacked me in the face again, knocking me to the floor. Spots swam before my eyes.

She swept out of the room, pushing her daughters before her, and slammed the door. The key clicked in the lock.

"No!" I shouted

I crawled to the door and pounded until my hands ached, but it didn't budge.

I was trapped. Locked in the attic, and all hope of rescuing Henri gone.

CHAPTER 26

"They're going to send me to gaol," I mumbled, resting my forehead against the door.

They would find out I was a woman. What would they do to me? Whatever it was, I would not save my brother or help Beatrice. I would never do...do anything for myself, either. When everything was lost to me, I realized that I had been hoping that someday, in the future, I would finally have time for the things I enjoyed. Traveling to new places, drawing, finding someone who would truly see me and cherish me. And now I would do none of them.

I went to the window and looked down, but it was a straight drop to the street far below. There was no way I could climb out.

"*I'm sorry.*" Beatrice came to rest next to me.

"It's not your fault," I said. "I only wanted to help. Help my brother, help you."

Had I ever helped Henri, though? He was not spoiled like

Frances, but I had built such a shelter around him—the walls so thick and windowless—that I'd left him naïve enough to fall into the smugglers' trap. And now, when I wasn't there to save him, what tools did he have to save himself?

Beatrice reached out as though she would seize my hand. *"You did help me, though. You gave me someone to talk to. I... I don't feel as lost as I did. Or as afraid. You've given me some answers."* She hesitated, then met my eyes. *"I'm just glad that someone cares. That even if I fade away, I'm not forgotten."*

"Never," I said fiercely.

Her eyes brightened. *"I can go with you to gaol! Then you won't be alone either."*

I managed a watery smile. "Thank you."

"If only other people could see me. I would scare off the smugglers who have your brother."

I nodded glumly, not able to respond past the lump in my throat. For all I knew, I was already too late to save Henri, and the smugglers had tossed him to a watery grave.

"Cousin Charles?" a small voice came through the door.

I scrambled to my feet. "Loretta?"

"Yes, it's me. I... I wanted to say that you were right. About Frances. She is awful. And Mother will never see how bad she's made it—how bad we all made it by pandering to her. I only hope I can escape with Mr. Hawke."

"I hope you can, too," I said. "You don't deserve this."

"Neither do you! You're always helping, and you never asked for anything for yourself. I know how that feels. I'm never allowed to ask for anything either. It's always about

Frances." Her voice hitched. "Well, now I'm doing something for both of us."

"What—" I began.

The lock clicked open.

"We're going out tonight to a ball," Loretta whispered. "As soon as we leave, escape to somewhere better than this. For both of our sakes!"

Her skirts rustled as she fled back down the stairs. I stared at the door. My route to freedom.

"What are you going to do?" Beatrice asked.

I had to think about that. I was not going to abandon my brother, but beyond that determination, I had no idea. One step at a time. One step toward being who I wanted to be.

"The first thing, is that I'm done being Charles."

I stripped out of my boys' clothing and put on one of Beatrice's old dresses. "Much better."

I felt a little closer to myself that way, though I might save the trousers in case I ever had the opportunity to tramp through fields and around ruins doing sketches.

Then there was nothing to do but listen for the Medfords to leave. I occupied myself by sketching. But this time, I didn't focus on the Revolution or on Lymouth. I drew some of the memories I had shared with Beatrice and Loretta, of my mother and traveling with my father and Henri. And then some of my dreams: my imaginings of Rome, a snug house nestled in a wild garden, whirling around a dance floor in the arms of a handsome man with red-gold hair.

Beatrice drifted downstairs and back again several times to report on the Medford's progress, and finally the carriage rumbled away from the house.

"Now?" Beatrice asked.

"Yes." I quickly packed a satchel with my sketchbook and a few things I might need. "First, we get our possessions back from Mrs. Medford."

Beatrice grinned. *"Really?"*

"Yes."

She checked that the way was clear, then we hurried for Mrs. Medford's room. The door swung open silently.

"Where would she keep it?" I asked myself, rummaging through the closet.

There was a jewelry box, but it was locked. No sign of my hard-earned coins.

"Over here!" Beatrice called, pointing to the dressing table.

There was her brooch, tossed casually aside. Mrs. Medford failed to see its value, probably thought the emeralds were only paste. I touched it gingerly. The clue to Beatrice's fate.

"Take it," Beatrice said. *"It must be worth ten pounds. You can trade it to the smugglers for your brother."*

I sighed. "Maybe. But not yet. We need it for you."

"For me?" Beatrice sighed. *"You have done so much, and I wasn't even thinking of what it might cost you."*

"Well, I want to help you," I said. And it was true. I'd never liked helping Frances, but Beatrice deserved justice, and I might be able to offer it. "You're my friend, and it's not fair that you're trapped this way. Someone in your household killed you."

"And someone covered it up," Beatrice said.

"Could it have been a servant?"

"Maybe," she said slowly. *"How can we find out?"*

"We need to confront your brother," I said. "Even if he didn't know about your murder at the time, he must know something about the servants."

"Where do we find him?"

"At the ball," I said. Inspiration struck. "I'll dress as you again."

"But Lord Treverton took the costume."

"He did. And we're going to get it back."

CHAPTER 27

I hurried through the dim streets, much more conspicuous in my dress than in my boy's clothing. I kept my head down and walked quickly, Beatrice sweeping ahead to warn me if anyone approached.

We reached the inn where Treverton had his rooms, and I realized Charlotte had another problem Charles did not: they would not let me in to see Treverton when I was dressed like a lady. It would be unthinkable.

I studied the windows, finding his.

"Can you see if he's in?" I asked Beatrice.

She nodded and drifted through the wall. She returned a few moments later. "He is sitting on his bed, looking forlorn."

Trying to decide which Medford girl to marry? My stomach twisted, but he had Beatrice's dress, and I needed it back. I picked up several pebbles and hurled them at the window, missing half the time.

After a few missiles hit home, he swung open the window.

"Carter?" he asked, his expression brightening. "Ah, but Charles no more, I see."

I bounced from foot to foot, glancing about to be sure no one saw me. "I need the dress—Miss Foley's costume."

His eyebrows drew together. "Why? No, never mind. Come up here before someone sees you." He reached a hand down.

I glanced at the front of the building. Luckily, the curtains on the bottom windows were closed. I managed to find some footholds on the façade's decorative brickwork, but climbing was much more difficult in a dress. Treverton stretched for me. I grabbed his hand, his grip sure and steadying. With his help, I scrambled up the side of the building and through his window, tumbling onto the floor in an unladylike heap.

I expected some crude comment from him about being in his bedchamber, but he only pulled Beatrice's costume from a clothes press. "Life is never dull with you around. Now, tell me why you need Miss Foley's costume. I won't be left out of the adventure."

I sighed, then explained to him about finding the brooch.

"You think her brother knows something?" Treverton said.

"The only way to find out is to confront him. I'll appear to him as Beatrice and demand he tell the truth."

"That's a scene I wouldn't want to miss," Treverton said with a grin.

Someone pounded at his front door. "Treverton?"

He rolled his eyes. "It's Hawke. I'll be rid of him."

And so, he left me hiding alone in his bedchamber. Hmm. A little awkward. I bundled up the dress.

"Yes, what's the fuss about?" Treverton asked at the front door.

"Quickly, shut the door. I'm glad I found you!" Hawke said, thumping into the front room.

"What's happened?" Treverton asked.

"They caught a boat of smugglers," Hawke said. "They're holding them in the gaol, waiting to hang every one of them —even a French boy who claims he was kidnapped."

Treverton was silent. I stood slowly, the room spinning around me. No, no, no. They could not have Henri. They could not hang Henri.

"There is more," Hawke said, his voice holding me to the room like an anchor, otherwise I might spin away. Or faint.

"Oh?" Treverton asked, his voice tight.

"They're pressuring the smuggler's captain to name his accomplices in town. He says the revenue men have to promise him protection, but he can tell them a story to make their eyes start from their heads—things much worse than smuggling. Things involving certain members of Society."

I leaned against the door. The smuggler couldn't mean me. But maybe it had something to do with Beatrice after all.

"And you're warning me?" Treverton asked. "You thought I was a part of this?"

"You're not?" Hawke asked. "Well, I'm glad to hear it. I did think you were involved. You've dabbled in a lot of shady things, and with members of Society mixed up in this business, I thought of you and of Lord Martin."

"Lord Martin! Am I as bad as he, then?" Treverton's voice was cold. Then he said more softly, "I suppose I truly have been unworthy."

"Well, when you put on that devil-may-care attitude, who knows what you get up to?" Hawke said. "Better to warn you and risk offending you, especially when the matter is urgent."

Yes, deathly urgent. I glanced down at the dress in my arms.

"*Go!*" Beatrice said. "*This is more important.*"

"Thank you," I mouthed.

I left the costume and my things and stumbled for the window, my hand on the papered wall for support. Fingers shaking, I lowered myself out the window, stumbling when I hit the ground.

What was I to do? They would be holding Henri in a local gaol. I had to find a way to free him before he was executed or transported. He wouldn't even have the option of turning king's evidence, since he didn't know anything about the smugglers' web of spies and agents.

"*How are you going to do it?*" Beatrice asked behind me.

"I don't know," I admitted. "I will have to examine the gaol."

Her forehead creased in concern.

"Don't bother trying to talk me out of this," I said. "I have already lost one family member unjustly imprisoned. I will not lose another."

She nodded. "*I was not going to try to stop you, only offer some information.*"

I raised an eyebrow, waiting for her to go on.

"The gaol is down the street. We toured it once. They keep the prisoners on the upper floor. The walls are quite solid, I'm afraid, but I don't think the bars on the windows are quite so sturdy."

I nodded, thinking that over.

She was silent for a long moment. *"Charlotte?"*

I looked over my shoulder. "Yes?"

"They can hang you even for associating with smugglers."

"They can hang me for many things, but they will not hang my brother."

And with that, I hurried into the night.

CHAPTER 28

The final sliver of the moon had not yet risen, and in the darkness, the nightwatchman was easy to avoid. I glanced back at Treverton's window and felt a surge of sorrow. Surely, only because I felt I was abandoning Beatrice to her in-between state. But I could not abandon my brother, and whether my plan worked or not, I would have to flee Lymouth once he was free. I winced when I realized I still had the brooch in the pocket under my skirts, but I couldn't go back now. At least Mrs. Medford and Frances didn't have it.

"Beatrice?" I whispered.

Nothing. She must have worn herself out again. I said a silent prayer for her and hurried for the gaol.

I watched the building and determined which room held the prisoners. It appeared they kept all the men together, which made this more dangerous. The window was on the upper floor of the building as Beatrice said, but it was not a terribly long drop to the ground, and I found some rope in a nearby stable. Enough to hang myself, no doubt. But Henri would escape.

I went below the window and gave a long whistle Henri would recognize from our time sneaking across the French countryside. The gaol was dark, but I could not imagine that he slept deeply in that place.

"Charlotte?" his voice called in the darkness, small and uncertain. Something in me almost broke at the sound.

"I'm here," I responded. "If I toss a rope up, can you catch it?"

"Yes."

It took a couple of tries, but I tossed the rope close enough for him to reach it. The hand that extended through the window grate was bony and pale.

"Tie it to the bars," I whispered. "Be ready to jump down."

I could barely see his gaunt face, but he nodded bravely and did as I asked him, tying the rope with a deftness that no doubt came from his time on the ship.

Now, the difficult part. The bars did not look tightly fitted, but I would not be strong enough to yank them loose, even using all my weight; if they were that weak, the smugglers would already have escaped. I was going to have to borrow a horse from the stable as well. That was probably going to attract attention.

"And what are you planning now?" a voice whispered behind me.

I gasped and turned to find Treverton there, a mask

covering his upper face and a holstered dueling pistol belted under his coat.

"What are you doing here?" I demanded in a hushed tone. "You are likely to be caught."

He grinned. "Then that will prove that I'm not entirely selfish. Though, I could probably bribe my way out of being hung." His smile faded. "I could not bribe your brother out of gaol, unfortunately. The magistrate wants the information the smugglers have too badly for the gaoler to part with them easily."

I stared at him. "You were going to buy Henri's freedom? Why didn't you tell me?"

"Firstly, because you ran off before I could speak to you. I tried giving a message to, uh, Beatrice, but I'm not sure she was still there. And secondly, I didn't know if my plan would work. And since it did not, here we are." He tugged the rope and looked up at the window. "You'll not be able to pull it free."

"I know. I was going to steal a horse."

"Blast it all, are you trying to be hanged? If you're not willing to think of your own well-being, at least consider how I will suffer when I have to break you out of gaol."

I rolled my eyes and whispered, "Do you have a better plan?"

His teeth flashed bright in the darkness, and he held something up. A chisel. "I borrowed this from a carpenter's shop. I'll return it in the morning, and he'll never be the wiser."

I shook my head, a mixture of shock and gratitude

twisted up inside me. "Your love of adventure is going to get you killed."

"Perhaps, but not tonight." He grinned again. "And I'm not doing this for a love of *adventure*."

He brushed a finger along my jaw, and my cheeks heated. I looked away. He should not tease me after he had been ashamed to be caught kissing me.

"Here," he said quietly. "Tie the chisel to the rope so they can haul it up." His hand brushed mine, sending a flash of warmth between us in the darkness.

The smugglers worked quickly and quietly to loosen the bars and pull them free, then just as quickly slid down the rope to the street. As soon as they touched the ground, they scattered into the night. One of them dropped the chisel for Treverton.

The captain stopped before me and looked over my dress, clearly confused. Then he shrugged. "I guess we'll call your debt even after all, *mademoiselle*."

I wanted to strangle him, but this was not the time.

Henri was one of the last ones down. He looked just as small as before, but more wiry, his eyes determined in his thin face as he climbed down the rope.

"Gaol break!" cried a voice from above. "They've escaped!"

I didn't even have to time to embrace my brother—just took his hand and ran for the outskirts of town. I was surprised to find Treverton running alongside of us. He could simply stroll off into the night, and no one would dare question him.

The sound of pounding feet approached, and shouts echoed through the streets.

"We need somewhere to hide," I panted.

"I know a place," Henri whispered. "One of the smugglers' caches."

"Take us there," I said.

Henri nodded and guided me through the dark outside of town. I quickly lost my way, but Henri had learned something from the smugglers. He dipped and dodged through hedgerows and trees, guiding us away from the shouting voices. His pace never faltered, though his breath came in ragged gasps.

The sea whispered and hissed nearby, and the ground turned rocky. I dropped Henri's hand, wavering to keep my balance, and I turned my ankle on a stone.

Treverton caught my elbow, keeping me upright. I wanted to shake him loose and tell him to hide somewhere else, to leave Henri and I to make our own way, but he kept his grip on me, kept me from slipping, so I let him guide me after Henri down a dark ravine.

The scents of damp soil and seawater and musty old leaves rolled around us. A fine mist chilled the air, and the rush of a waterfall covered the sound of our footsteps. We went down a set of steps that seemed to be carved from the ancient stone. A deeper darkness loomed in front of us.

I fumbled out and grabbed Henri's shirt to keep him close. "Where are we?" I whispered.

Treverton answered. "I think we're below the ruins of the old Lymouth monastery."

"It's an ancient crypt," Henri said. "Dug into the cliffside."

I groaned. I did not want to deal with more ghosts. But even less I wanted to meet the men hunting us.

I followed Henri into the darkness.

I felt my way down the passage, keeping my fingers on the damp stone walls. They felt too smooth for a natural cave. As Henri said, it must have been carved out by people at some point in the past.

We moved farther in, and I imagined the weight of all the earth overhead. Cold water dripped down on me, making my teeth chatter. The crypt might be ancient, but I feared it would not hold together for much longer.

A hiss sounded in front of me, and a light jumped into view. It wasn't very bright, but I winced and shielded my eyes. Treverton did the same.

"Sorry," Henri said, holding up an oil lamp. He wasn't whispering anymore, but his voice sounded odd and muted in the crypt.

The lantern threw long, wavering shadows on the niches in the wall, and I was very careful not to look at them. At the bodies crumbling to dust while they awaited their call to resurrection.

Treverton had no such reservations. He peered with interest into the resting places lining the wall like bunks on a ship.

"This place is ancient—maybe even older than the monastery," he said. "I'm surprised more people don't know about it."

"A lot of locals probably do," Henri said. "But they benefit from the smuggling, so they don't say anything." There was a bitter edge to his voice.

"Oh, Henri!" I hurried to embrace him, feeling the sharp angles of his ribcage. "Are you unharmed?"

He was still pale, and dark circles highlighted his weary eyes, but he stood straighter than I remembered.

He snorted. "At first, they worked me to the bone. They might have worked me to death, but..." He grinned. "I found that all of Father's boring lessons were actually useful. I could read their maps and the stars, help them navigate. I became pretty skilled at predicting the weather, too. It earned me some relief from the hard labor. Probably saved my life. That, and they were counting on you bringing the money." He gave me a curious look.

"I had almost all of it, but it was taken from me. It doesn't matter now, though. We're both free."

"Well," said a voice from the entrance, "We'll have to talk about that. I might charge you bed and board for staying in my hidey hole."

We all turned to see the captain standing there, looking smug.

"I don't think so." Treverton pulled the pistol from under his coat.

The captain laughed and flashed his own gun. "Oh, do you think you're the only one armed? But it needn't come to that."

"I set you free," I said. "You told me the debt was paid."

"Yours is, but I never let an opportunity pass," the captain said, glancing at Treverton. "A lord consorting with criminals? That must be worth something to hush up."

Treverton laughed. "You sadly misunderstand me if you think you can blackmail me. What do I care for rumors? And who will take your word against mine?"

"Oh, yes, I know your reputation, *Lord* Treverton," the captain said. "But that's only a courtesy title, ain't it? Your grandfather the earl holds your purse strings, and you'll dance when he pulls them. What would he pay to have this scandal hushed up? You nobs and your Society play vicious games, I've learned."

His eyes flicked, ever so briefly, to one of the crypts.

I followed where he had looked. A scrap of fabric hung from the niche, mildewy but still recognizable. Beatrice's muslin gown.

CHAPTER 29

"Beatrice!" I cried out and started forward, but Treverton's hand on my arm stopped me.

I almost shrugged him off, but then I remembered that Beatrice had been gone a year. This cold Beatrice turning to dust in a crypt was not the one who had become my friend, and I did not need to see the grim details.

Treverton leaned closer to her, then pulled back quickly. "Yes, I do believe we have found Miss Foley."

"You know that dead girl?" Henri asked. "But how?"

I ignored Henri's question and whirled on the captain. "You murdered her!"

He grimaced. "You think I want that kind of attention? All of Society looking for her last year? No, the one who killed her knew this place and dropped her here. I wasn't happy to find her body stuffed in my crypt, either, but I could hardly report it, and he knew it."

"Then who did this?" Treverton asked, his voice cold.

"Your folks. Someone in Society. I'm not naming names without protection. But it's a gentleman what likes to take a firm hand in things, and he did."

A chill went over me. Mr. Foley guided his ship with a firm hand. "Gentleman?" I looked to Treverton. "Mr. Foley?"

His mouth turned into a hard line, and anger made his green eyes flash. "If so, he's a worse cad than I ever suspected." Treverton leveled a cold look at the captain. "You knew where she was all the time her loved ones were searching for her. You helped her murderer cover his tracks. You may not have killed her, but I would like to see you hanged for your hand in this."

The captain shifted, reaching for his gun, but Treverton had his dueling pistol out in a heartbeat.

"Not quick enough," Treverton said. "I may let you walk out of here tonight, but neither myself nor my grandfather will ever hear a word from you about blackmail. Or anything else."

The captain grunted, then he smiled ruefully and let his hands rest by his side. "Deal. I'm giving up on Lymouth anyway. But you can't blame a fellow for taking a gamble."

I glared at him. He *had* set Henri up with his gambling tricks.

Treverton made a motion with his pistol, and the captain scurried away.

"You've been busy," Henri said.

I turned to him. "I've been earning money to rescue you, too."

"I know." He bit his lip. "I knew you wouldn't abandon me, and in the beginning, that was all that kept me going.

Then I was angry that you didn't save me immediately, and I imagined you having a grand time in the city with our cousins—"

I snorted, but he went on.

"And I was envious and...and furious. But then I realized that I had never seen you have a grand time. Never seen you do anything for yourself. And I was finding that I could do some things for *myself*. Someday, I might like to be a navigator for a ship. An honest one, though."

"You've grown up," I said.

"Yes. I think I have. I just needed to be tossed on my ear to figure things out. Not that I blame you for protecting me. I know I wouldn't have made it all these years without you. But now... well, I don't understand what happened to your friend. But I hope you can catch the person who hurt her. And find some happiness for yourself, too."

I glanced at Treverton, who gave me an I-told-you-so smile.

"We have to confirm what Mr. Foley knew," I said.

Treverton nodded and secured his pistol. "Lead on, my lady."

"I'll hide out in the woods for a time and meet up with you later at, uh..." Henri trailed off, at a loss.

Treverton handed him a calling card. "Find me. I'll direct you to your sister. After tonight, her location may be a little unsettled."

Henri nodded and took the card.

Treverton looked at me. "Well?"

"It is time for me to dress as Beatrice once more," I said. "We have a ball to attend."

CHAPTER 30

I made Treverton wait outside his rooms while I pulled Beatrice's dress over my own, prepared in case I needed to shed it quickly once again. Then I placed the brown wig atop my short hair.

Beatrice swam into focus in front of me, looking worn and especially ethereal.

"You returned! Did you rescue your brother?"

"Yes, he is safe." The words were so sweet, I could hardly believe they were real.

"You've learned something more."

I took a slow breath. "I've seen your body. You're buried in the crypt of an old monastery by the cliffs."

"Oh! Was it...was it terrible?"

"I didn't look closely. It's a peaceful place, though. Your body doesn't appear to have been disturbed or desecrated."

"That's...that's good news, I suppose. Did it tell you anything about my killer?"

"He was likely a gentleman connected with the smugglers," I said as gently as I could.

Beatrice drifted around me in a circle. *"Could it have been my brother, then? I'm sure he bought smuggled goods. Oh! I don't know what to think."*

I watched her with sympathy. "I don't know either, but we're going to the ball to find out."

"Thank you," Beatrice said, her voice wavering. *"Whatever…whatever happens tonight, I want you to know that I appreciate it. One good thing about my being trapped as a ghost is that we were able to become friends."*

"Yes, I am glad of that at least," I said quietly. "It's the strangest thing to ask, but…but if you're able to move on, if you see my father or mother, will you let them know that we're going to be fine, Henri and I? And that I hope they are together and at peace."

"Of course," Beatrice said. *"Oh, I wish I could embrace you. But I have to ask one more thing of you as well, even after all you've done for me."*

"What is it?"

"Live. See the world. Dance at parties. Keep making your sketches. Do the things I never had the chance to do."

I nodded, my throat too tight to answer. I wished I could embrace her as well, but I would do what I could for her. And for myself.

"Come, we have a ball to attend," Beatrice said.

I tied on the mask and stepped out of the room. Treverton moved closer, his eyes fixed on mine. He reached a hand for my face, and I tensed. But he only adjusted the mask.

"If not for your eyes, I wouldn't know it was you," he said.

"Good," I managed, though my voice was strangely breathy. "That's the idea."

He nodded and offered his arm. "This way."

He snuck me out the back of the lodgings, and we hurried through the dark streets, avoiding members of the watch searching for the escaped smugglers. I hoped none questioned us, because we could not say that we had seen nothing.

We reached the house hosting the ball, and my stomach crawled like it was filled with ants. Not since fleeing Paris had I been so nervous.

"You have the brooch?" Treverton asked.

I nodded.

"I'll go in first and circulate with the crowd," Treverton said. "You come in and confront Foley."

"Yes," I said.

He stared at me for a moment, and I couldn't break from his green eyes. Then, he leaned down for a swift kiss on my cheek.

"You're not alone," he whispered in my ear. "I will be watching over you."

With that, he was gone, and I was left only with a lingering warmth on my face and a regret that I could not put on my former role as a proper young lady as easily as I pulled on Beatrice's costume.

"*Do you know what you'll say to my brother?*" Beatrice asked, breaking through my confused thoughts.

"I'll improvise, depending on how he reacts."

She nodded and fisted her hands against her translucent skirts.

I waited several minutes, then I found my way through the garden and into the ballroom.

As before, people stopped to stare at me. More, since this was not a costume ball. This time, though, Mr. Foley was in attendance, and many eyes turned to find his reaction as well.

He went pale, and then his face reddened with anger. He stalked toward me. The room went quiet, the musicians waiting to start another song.

"This is in poor taste," Foley said. "You're not welcome here."

Beatrice put a hand on my arm, and I would have sworn I felt her touching me, almost felt what she was feeling.

"Do you know me then, brother?" I asked, not sure if the words were mine or hers.

"You are not my sister," he said, though his voice shook a little. "My sister is dead."

"Are you certain?" I asked. "Is that because you know where my body lies?"

"My sister is gone," he said weakly.

"Not so far from here, though," I said. "My body lies in the crypt near the cliffs, in the same dress I wore the day I died."

Murmurs ran through the room.

Now, the color had drained entirely from Foley's face. "No."

"Do you remember that day, brother?" I held out my

hand and revealed the brooch. "I still need to return this to Mother."

Frances gave a gasp of protest, and I wondered for a moment if she would try to claim it. But I whipped my gaze to her, and she cowered. No, even she would not dare lie to a dead woman, and she couldn't be certain I was her cousin.

I turned back to Foley. "Do you remember?"

"My sister disappeared," he said weakly.

Beatrice released my arm and drifted forward. *"I never went anywhere, though. I've been here all along. And...I almost remember."*

Foley's eyes widened further, and he looked around. He heard her this time. He couldn't see her, but he heard her.

"What happened to me, brother?" she asked. *"What happened on those stairs?"*

"Nothing!" he said. "Stop this! You were always a pest. You didn't do as you were supposed to do."

The crowd shifted and murmured. They couldn't hear Beatrice. They only heard Foley's frantic reply.

"Did I interfere with your smuggling?"

"I was only looking out for our family. We needed money —always more money for clothes and parties and carriages. And you...you wouldn't stay in your place. First your fixation with Hawke, and then you wanted to run out into the garden."

"Where the smugglers were coming to meet you," I said.

His eyes darted back to me. "You are not my sister!"

He reached forward as if he would grab my mask. Beatrice stepped between us, and his hand touched her. He hissed and grasped his fingers.

"So cold!" he gasped.

"I will never rest until you tell the truth," I said. "What did you do to Beatrice Foley?"

He clasped his hand. "I didn't mean to hurt her. She wouldn't obey me, and we argued. She...she fell."

Beatrice gasped. *"I remember. I didn't fall. You shook me. Shook me so hard it rattled my brain. And when you let go, I tumbled down the stairs."*

"I didn't mean for you to fall!" he said. "I just wanted you to do as I said, you ungrateful brat. And you had to go and tumble down and break your neck."

The room gasped. Foley blinked and looked around, as if only now remembering that he had an audience.

"But you hid my body," I pushed. "You didn't want anyone to see the bruises on my arms and know that you had shaken me and made me fall."

"Why couldn't you just behave!" Foley screamed.

"You," Beatrice said, *"were a terrible brother!"*

She shoved him, and he fell to the ground, shivering and sobbing.

Treverton moved forward through the crowd. "I believe we need to call a magistrate. And send a party to check the crypt."

In the bustle and confusion, I darted out of the hot room into the cool night air. Making certain everyone was distracted by Treverton and Foley, I wiggled out of Beatrice's costume and carefully nestled it in the shadows of an overgrown hawthorn. Maybe someday I could return it to her mother, who now had two reasons to grieve.

For the moment, I was myself again, and I had a better idea of who that was.

I looked for Beatrice. She lingered behind me. The stars showed through her faint figure.

"Thank you," she said, her voice little more than the whisper in the breeze.

My chest tightened. She was leaving me. "Are you at peace?"

"Yes. I remember it all now. I am sad but...but I have a sense that all will be made right somehow. There is light all around me, and I can rest."

"I will miss you," I whispered.

"I don't think I will be terribly far away, even if you can't see me anymore." She smiled. *"Live for me, and look for me in the twinkle of the stars and the light dancing on the water."*

"Of course," I choked out.

Beatrice faded completely, and her voice breathed over me. *"Until we meet again, my friend."*

CHAPTER 31

I sat on a bench and let the warm tears stream down my cheeks. Beatrice wanted me to find happiness, but she couldn't begrudge me a moment of mourning. It was too quiet in the garden. Lonely. But I was glad Beatrice was at peace. And Henri would make his own way once we were settled. That meant I had to decide what I wanted for me.

An image of Treverton flashed through my mind, but I shook it away. He was destined for one of the Medford girls —or at least for someone his grandfather approved of. Someone he wasn't ashamed to kiss.

I looked up to the stars, remembering how my father had studied them for hours They were beautiful, but my answers weren't there like his were. Drawing, though. That was something I did enjoy. Not always pictures of the Revolution or the stormy sea, but the moments of light and beauty breaking through the darkness. Maybe Charlotte could do as well at that as Charles. I could make my way on my art—and I would do it as myself and not as someone else.

"There he is!" Frances said behind me.

I turned to see her with Mrs. Medford, Loretta, and the revenue man.

My knees went watery. So much for Charlotte. Henri had escaped the noose, but I would not.

I stood slowly. I didn't regret helping Henri. Or Beatrice. But I wished I'd never spent a moment caring what my treacherous cousin thought of me.

Frances pointed. "He's dressed as a girl, but that's the same boy who pretended to be our cousin and robbed me. He's a French spy!"

"What is the meaning of this?" I drew myself up and allowed my French accent to roll off my tongue. No reason to hide it now, and the revenue man had only heard me trying to sound English.

The revenue man examined me then looked at my cousin. "This person appears to me to be female."

A few people had trickled into the garden to watch the drama unfold. They laughed at this statement.

Mrs. Medford stepped up to glare at me, her eyes resting on the side of my face, which was probably developing a bruise where she had struck me. She smiled coldly.

I returned her glare.

"This person is an expert at deception," Mrs. Medford said. "He—or she—took advantage of my generosity and my daughters' naivety."

The revenue man stared hard at my face. "There is something familiar about her."

"There ought to be," a man said from the back of the crowd.

Treverton!

The crush parted for him, and he came to stand beside me.

"My lord," Mrs. Medford said. "I'm sorry we allowed you to be deceived by this person."

"Whatever are you talking about?" Treverton slipped his arm through mine and stared down at Mrs. Medford. "Miss Charlotte Carter has not deceived me."

"Miss *Carter*?" The revenue man asked. "I understood the person in question was a *Cartier*."

Treverton raised his quizzing glass and leveled it at the man. "Cartier? Wasn't that the Medford's French tutor? Entertaining lad. Good at cards."

"He claimed to be our cousin!" Frances said, her voice rising in pitch. "And that's him! He had the dress. The red slipper. He fooled everyone!"

Treverton turned his quizzing glass on Frances. "I don't pretend to keep track of all your cousins, but I happen to know that this *lady* is Miss Charlotte Carter, the granddaughter of your grandfather's sister. That lady—her grandmother—was also a good friend of my grandfather, the earl. I have been corresponding with him, and he was delighted to hear that Miss Carter, and her brother Henri, have arrived safely from France. And I am delighted as well."

He smiled down at me, all his coldness vanishing for a moment.

Frances's eyes widened, and she stared at me, her face reddening and her mouth moving in fury.

Treverton went on. "It is a shame if you were taken in by a charlatan who pretended to be a cousin. That is what comes of being too generous, I suppose."

Loretta spoke up. "I always thought there was something odd about that lad." She met my eyes and smiled. "But I am glad to meet my real cousin at last. And hope to know her better someday soon?"

I smiled back at her. "Enchantée, mademoiselle."

Mrs. Medford listened to the whole exchange with a face of iron. She snapped out a handkerchief and dabbed at a dry eye. "Yes, it is monstrous what these people will do. Pretending to be an aristocrat. Above their station. They will fall at the last."

She fixed me with a gaze of daggers before turning away. "Come, girls. No need to make a scene."

Frances gasped. "Mother! You are not going to leave that...that *person* hanging there on Lord Treverton's arm! He is supposed to be for me. You promised I would be a countess!"

Gasps and titters ran through the crowd. I winced for Frances.

Crimson lit Mrs. Medford's face. "Frances! You are clearly overwrought by the events of this evening. Come along."

"But Mother—"

"Now!"

Frances stuttered and hesitated between her mother and me. For a moment, I thought she might try to claw my eyes out. But she burst into tears and swooned to the ground.

The crowd only stared, a few in the back chuckling. Then Mr. Hawke stepped forward to lift her. Frances fluttered her eyes open to smile sweetly at him, but his gaze was focused on Loretta.

"My dear Miss Loretta, where shall I take your poor sister?"

"I think we had best go home," Loretta said, smiling at her sweetheart.

Frances burst into fresh tears as Hawke carried her away.

The crowd dispersed, most following the Medfords to see if there was to be a third act to the night's drama.

The revenue man watched me for a moment longer, a suspicious glint in his eye, then he glanced at Treverton and turned his back on me.

Soon, I was alone with Treverton.

"They have arrested Foley," Treverton said, releasing my arm. "Though they need an alternate place to hold him, as it seems the gaol experienced a recent escape." The amusement faded from his voice. "And they will give Miss Foley a more proper burial."

I tried to smile. "I am glad to hear it."

"You left your sketchbook. I wanted to return it." He held the book out, open to the drawing of me dancing with him.

I flushed and took the book quickly, snapping it shut. "A lady's sketchbook is private."

"That sketch gave me hope that I had not bungled everything beyond repair, so I cannot quite regret prying." He raised an eyebrow. "And are you settled on being a lady again?"

"You may not think I've ever been a lady, the way you... you misused me in that alcove—"

"I seem to recall you 'misusing' me with equal enthusiasm," he said, grinning. "And I have never forgotten you are a lady. I certainly would not have kissed a French tutor. Nor would I have written so glowingly of any French tutor to my grandfather."

I gasped. "Your...grandfather?"

"My grandfather." He rolled his eyes. "The earl that everyone is so in awe of. I didn't lie to the Medfords. As fond as Grandfather was of Mr. Medford's father, he also remembers your own father's mother as a dear friend."

"Does he?" My mind whirled. "I never met my English grandmother."

"Your grandmother, their grandfather—your entire family saw him through difficult days. When I could not find a lady who interested me above the others, he, uh, *encouraged* me to marry into the family of his old friends. He assumed they would be as good as their forebearers. Ha! I'm grateful he'll never meet Frances Medford. But he was delighted to hear a slightly abridged version of your story."

My heartbeat quickened, but I knew he couldn't be serious. "You are trifling with me again. You were afraid to be seen with me."

"Only afraid that I had endangered you." He ran his hands through his hair. "Oh, my darling. I truly have been unworthy. If I cannot convince you that I have a heart, then surely no one will believe it. But I never wanted to trifle with you. I wanted—still want—to marry you."

Hope welled inside me, but I didn't dare let it loose. "I have no dowry."

"I don't care, and neither will Grandfather. I am rich enough for both of us."

"I am a black sheep."

Treverton laughed. "And so am I. They will say you were the making of me. They might not be wrong."

A familiar weight settled on my shoulders, and I drooped under it. Would Treverton expect me to always be the serious, steady one while he was carefree? I liked the idea of listening to his troubles and sharing his burdens, but I would never again try to carry all the responsibilities myself.

"I will not be a silent wife, always covering for your follies."

"Good heavens, I would hope not. How dull! If anything, I hope you engage in a bit of folly alongside me." His fingers brushed down my arm, leaving a trail of goosebumps.

I raised my chin. "I want to continue my sketches. Even display them."

He took my hand and kissed it, his lips lingering on my knuckles. "I will buy a gallery for you."

I almost agreed, but common sense stopped me. "No, I want to succeed on my own. I need to do it for myself."

"If you insist. Though, you have shown me that occasionally playing the white knight is enjoyable, so you must remember that you don't have to do *everything* alone."

"Not anymore," I said, and the weight slipped again from my shoulders.

Treverton pulled me closer and kissed me. I kissed him back, enthusiastically, neither of us caring if anyone saw.

EPILOGUE

I arranged the last of my drawings, inspecting them carefully. This one showed the chaos in the Place de la Révolution as a tumbrel of victims rolled toward their doom. To one side of it stood an image of how I remembered Paris before the bloodshed, and on the other side, a sketch of what I hoped my dear city would someday be again. I stepped back to study the effect—a moment of deep darkness in a history also filled with light and hope.

"Perfect," Treverton said behind me.

I turned to smile at my husband. "It should be. I've been working on it for hours."

"I was talking about you," he said, leaning down for a kiss.

"Ha!" I kissed him back, then gave him a playful push. "Don't put me on too high a pedestal. It will hurt when I fall off."

"I would never. But you have arranged everything beautifully."

I smoothed my dress over my growing belly—a development which had further endeared me to the earl. But his opinion wasn't the one that worried me at the moment. My hands trembled slightly. "I am terrified that people will hate it. Women don't often paint such scenes."

"You are a future countess. None will dare speak against you."

I pursed my lips. "I want no false praise. I wish Henri were here. He would tell me the truth."

My brother had grown stronger under the watchful eye of my new Grandpapa, the earl, and then elected to go off to school. Henri was perfectly happy there with the other scholars, though he sent his regrets that he could not see my art show. Loretta would attend with her beloved Hawke, but even freed from Frances and Mrs. Medford, Loretta remained too sweet and shy to say anything negative about my drawings.

"You know I am blisteringly honest," Treverton said. "Your work is skillful and moving. There will be some who don't care for it, but it is not your job to make everyone happy—only to capture the scenes you want the world to know and remember."

I glanced over at the picture of the bronze angel whose face reminded me of my mother—returned as a gift from Loretta and Hawke. Beside it was a portrait I had drawn of Beatrice, the young lady I had never known in life, but who had become a dear friend. Her eyes seemed to sparkle from the paper.

I smiled at Treverton. "I did not know I had married such a wise husband."

He pulled me into an embrace. "Then I am at an advantage. Because I always knew what a treasure I had when I found you."

"When you were drunk and thought I was a boy on the streets?" I asked.

He laughed. "No, the first time I saw through your disguise at the ball."

"I'm so glad you did," I said.

And I proved it with a kiss.

ALSO BY E.B. WHEELER

British Fiction:

Born to Treason

The Royalist's Daughter

The Haunting of Springett Hall

Wishwood (Westwood Gothic)

Moon Hollow (Westwood Gothic)

A Proper Dragon (Dragons of Mayfair 1)

An Elusive Dragon (Dragons of Mayfair 2)

A Subtle Dragon (Dragons of Mayfair 3)

Cruel Magic (Iron & Thorns 1)

Wild Magic (Irons & Thorns 2)

Utah Fiction:

No Peace with the Dawn (with Jeffery Bateman)

Letters from the Homefront (Utah at War)

Balm for the Heart (Utah at War)

Bootleggers and Basil (in *The Pathways to the Heart*)

Blood in a Dry Town (Tenny Mateo Mystery)

A Company of Bones (Tenny Mateo Mystery)

Nonfiction:

Utah Women: Pioneers, Poets & Politicians

ACKNOWLEDGMENTS

Writers are often introverts, but creating a book is a team effort. Thank you to my critique groups, The Writers' Cache and UPSSEFW, and especially to Keri and Lauren for their thoughtful feedback and support, and to my beta readers Dan, Karen, Laura, and Sharolyn for their insights. And as always, thank you to my family and to my husband for his unfailing support.

ABOUT THE AUTHOR

E.B. Wheeler is the author of over a dozen books of history, historical fiction, and historical fantasy, including Whitney Award finalists *Born to Treason* and *A Proper Dragon,* and YA Fantasy Whitney Award winner *Cruel Magic,* as well as short stories, magazine articles, and scripts for educational software programs. She has a B.A. in history with an English minor from BYU and graduate degrees in history and landscape architecture from Utah State University. In addition to writing, she sometimes consults about historic preservation and teaches history, and she loves gardening, folk music, reading, and exploring the West with her husband and kids.

Printed in the USA
CPSIA information can be obtained
at www.ICGtesting.com
CBHW081710190724
11847CB00008B/344